"It's my first hon

"My first time being a ~~s~~ but failed. "That's right, ~~isn't it. I'm on the list.~~

"You're the only person I'm sure is innocent. We were together the whole time."

"What about the others?"

"It's possible there was someone else." But not likely. "Does the castle have surveillance cameras?"

"It does." She turned to face him. "There must have been a reason you brought me into this room. Why?"

"I need for you to wrangle the guests and employees. Make sure nobody leaves. When my deputies get here, point them in this direction."

"I can handle that."

Somehow, he'd known that he could count on her. "For now, I'll stay here in the bedroom to make sure nobody disturbs the scene."

"Shouldn't be hard." She jabbed her thumb over her shoulder to indicate the door. "That's the only way in or out."

And that door had been locked.

COLD CASE COLORADO

—

USA TODAY Bestselling Author

CASSIE MILES

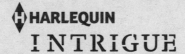

HARLEQUIN

INTRIGUE

To Rick and fond memories of driving through the mountains
looking for castles.

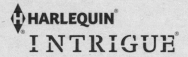

ISBN-13: 978-1-335-28449-5

Cold Case Colorado

Recycling programs
for this product may
not exist in your area.

This edition published by arrangement with Harlequin Books S.A.

For questions and comments about the quality of this book,
please contact us at CustomerService@Harlequin.com.

Harlequin Enterprises ULC
22 Adelaide St. West, 40th Floor
Toronto, Ontario M5H 4E3, Canada
www.Harlequin.com

Printed in U.S.A.

Cassie Miles, a *USA TODAY* bestselling author, lives in Colorado. After raising two daughters and cooking tons of macaroni and cheese for her family, Cassie is trying to be more adventurous in her culinary efforts. She's discovered that almost anything tastes better with wine. When she's not plotting Harlequin Intrigue books, Cassie likes to hang out at the Denver Botanic Gardens near her high-rise home.

Books by Cassie Miles

Harlequin Intrigue

Mountain Midwife
Sovereign Sheriff
Baby Battalion
Unforgettable
Midwife Cover
Mommy Midwife
Montana Midwife
Hostage Midwife
Mountain Heiress
Snowed In
Snow Blind
Mountain Retreat
Colorado Wildfire
Mountain Bodyguard
Mountain Shelter
Mountain Blizzard
Frozen Memories
The Girl Who Wouldn't Stay Dead
The Girl Who Couldn't Forget
The Final Secret
Witness on the Run
Cold Case Colorado

Visit the Author Profile page at Harlequin.com.

CAST OF CHARACTERS

Vanessa Whitman—Broke, unemployed and homeless after her father's death, she retreats to the Whitman Castle in the mountains after being harassed by a stalker. She discovers a new career as a ghostwriter.

Ty Coleman—After years on the Aspen Ski Patrol and Mountain Search and Rescue, Ty is elected sheriff of a small county near Aspen. The murder at Whitman Castle is his first homicide.

Simon Markham—Twelve years ago, Simon, a celebrity chef, lost his wife, Dorothy—Vanessa's aunt—under mysterious circumstances. Simon inherited the castle.

Dorothy Whitman Markham—Twelve years ago, she was declared dead by suicide. But not everyone believes Dorothy took her own life.

Keith Gable—Simon's partner developed his gourmet restaurant into a fast-food franchise and made a boatload of money.

Bethany Whitman Burke—Died from blunt force trauma in Simon's bedroom suite.

Lowell Burke—The husband of the murder victim is a lawyer.

Chapter One

Clouds shifted across the moonlit sky, creating ghostly shadows. Vanessa Whitman faced the graveyard, unafraid. She welcomed the spirits from her past, including her father who had been cremated only six days ago. When it came to sorting out her family heritage, she'd take all the help she could get, be it messages from the dead or a lawyer's brief.

She slipped through a narrow break in the border hedge at the far side of the 165-acre cemetery on the west side of Denver. The tall wrought iron gates at the front entrance had been locked an hour ago. After dark, visitors were supposed to check in, but that was a rule she had to break.

Frozen in place, she scanned the irregular rows of tombstones, grave markers and statues of guardian angels. Nobody else was here. Spring lilacs in full bloom scented the crisp night air. A breeze rustled the new leaves on poplars and aspens.

Clouds parted, and a shaft of moonlight pointed the way. She trod carefully across the carpet of grass. In her hands, she carried a Mason jar half-filled with a portion of her father's ashes that she'd taken from his urn. Her intention was to scatter Dad at the side-by-side plots he'd purchased when Mom passed away fifteen years ago.

The cemetery caretakers would most certainly *not* approve of her plan, but Vanessa couldn't afford to follow protocol. There was an internment fee, and she didn't have enough ready cash to pay right now. Sure, she could wait or make other arrangements or borrow the money, but she wanted to honor Dad's last request. And she wanted to do it now, right now.

For the past four years, he'd been dying from colon cancer and the many agonizing complications that went along with the disease, which meant that he and Vanessa had had plenty of time to discuss the final question: What to do with his remains? He'd wanted to leave a trace of himself in the far-flung corners of the Earth from the peak of Mount Everest to the lowest depth of the Mariana Trench. She'd convinced him to accept a more doable plan, scattering some of his ashes in the mountains where he grew up, some in the ocean to symbolize his many journeys and another portion here at the gravesite of his soul mate.

She halted in front of her mother's marker—a bronze plaque planted flat in the earth. A memory of her mother filled her mind. Vanessa always wished she looked more like Mom, with her delicate features and dark hair. Instead, she took after Dad, with his unruly honey-colored hair, his broad smile and freckles.

Her mother's plaque read *Margaret Whitman, beloved wife and mother*, followed by her birth date and the date—fifteen years ago—when she passed away. When Vanessa had the money, she'd have her father's matching plaque inscribed *John Joseph Whitman, husband, father, traveler and poet*, followed by the dates.

A car door slammed.

Startled, she shot a glance toward the entrance and saw no one coming through. Nor did she see vehicles on the narrow roads that meandered through the cemetery. The car must have stopped beyond the hedge. *No-*

body here. And yet a shudder rattled down her spine. Not scared but apprehensive, she sensed the presence of a watcher. Could it be the creep who had been following her for days? She waited for him to show himself. *Nothing.* He wasn't here.

She knelt in the grass before Mom's marker. Earlier today at a small memorial in the university chapel, she'd recited Dad's favorite Dylan Thomas poem. He would have been proud of the way she'd maintained her composure. That was then. And now? Tears sloshed behind her eyelids and spilled down her cheeks.

She set the Mason jar on the ground, kissed her fingertips and touched the bronze plaque as though she could reassure Mom. These tears were about more than sadness. She was also glad that her father's suffering was over. Sorrow, anger and...tension. She wiped at her eyes with the sleeve of her sweatshirt. Her future was as bleak as a moonscape. She'd quit her job teaching high school English to care for Dad and had made no plans for future employment. Every penny of her savings and Dad's as well was spent. The flood of medical bills had wiped out everything. Their properties were repossessed. All their assets were gone. Mom would have said it was impossible for her to be broke because the Whitmans had always been a superrich family.

A thread of anger wove through her fears. Her charming father had been wildly irresponsible. To finance his travels, he'd sold off artwork and property. She should have monitored his spending, grounded him, refused to pay for one last trip to Bali to watch the purple sunset behind the tiered pagodas and swaying palm trees. But she couldn't deny him.

John Joseph Whitman had died with a smile on his face and that meant the world to her. She unscrewed the lid on the Mason jar and poured a few ounces of Dad's remains into her palm. The ashes and tiny fragments of bone seemed to burn. Quickly, she sprinkled them around her mother's grave.

When she heard what sounded like someone walking on gravel, her gaze swiveled. This part of the cemetery was relatively new with more plaques in the ground than upright tombstones. For thirty feet in all directions, her view was uninterrupted. She saw nobody but felt her stalker was near. Anticipating the worst, she'd come prepared. In the pocket of her sweatshirt was a container of pepper spray.

The first time she'd seen her stalker was a couple of months ago, late at night. He'd been on the street outside the hospice, wearing a black cap and ski mask. He'd called her name, then raised his arm and pointed at her. The creep didn't come close enough for her to get a good look, just a general impression that he was average height and weight. She'd leaped into her car and driven home.

Now and again, she'd caught other glimpses but was too exhausted to do anything. When her apartment was broken into, she called the police. After a cursory look around, they'd found no evidence. Nothing had been stolen. They suggested that she stay with friends or family for a few days. That was when she'd contacted her wealthy Uncle Simon Markham who lived near Aspen. Vanessa had swallowed her pride and asked for money. To her surprise, Simon had stepped up and paid for a private suite in a nursing facility for her and her father.

Still kneeling at Mom's marker, she emptied the ashes from the Mason jar into the grass. Now Mom and Dad would be together forever. Vanessa flashed on a wishful vision of them holding hands in a rose garden, surrounded by love and beauty.

Their ordeal was over. And hers had just begun.

Behind her back, she heard the scrape of a boot against stone. Night birds took flight. When she whipped around, she saw a dark figure, dodging among the headstones and moving in her direction. For a moment, she lost sight of him in the shadows.

Why, why, why was he coming after her? Anger melted her fear and stirred her blood. Scrambling to her feet, she yelled, "Leave me alone."

"Vanessa." The breeze carried her name. "Vanessa, I won't hurt you."

"Don't come any closer." How dumb did he think she was? "Stay back."

He showed himself. Only thirty feet away from her, he was dressed in dark colors and wore a black ski mask. With long strides, he approached. "Vanessa, Vanessa."

"No," she yelled at him. "Get back."

She cocked her arm and threw the Mason jar at him. The glass jar thumped against his chest. A lucky shot! He stumbled, then regained his balance. "You little bitch!"

With her pepper spray in her hand, she

charged at him and aimed at his mask and his eyes. Screaming in pain, he sank to the ground.

She took off running. Her feet barely touched the grass as she darted through the graves to the break in the border hedge. Looking over her shoulder, she didn't see him coming after her but didn't slow her pace until she reached her car and jumped inside.

She slammed the car into gear and peeled away from the curb. At the corner, she turned left. After six more blocks, her little sedan merged into traffic. Was she safe? Would she ever be safe again?

In the distance, the mountains created solid ramparts against the night sky. Like a fortress, that rugged terrain would protect her. The implacable Rocky Mountains were where the story of the Whitman family began. Dad had wanted a portion of his ashes to be scattered amid those majestic peaks where he grew up.

She reached over and patted the urn that held the rest of his ashes. Riding in the passenger seat, it was held in place by the seat belt.

"Don't worry, Dad. I'm taking you home."

Chapter Two

Vanessa leaned back in the swivel chair behind the long library table with carved legs and took stock. It had been four months since she left Denver. As far as she could tell, her stalker hadn't followed her to Uncle Simon's sixteen-bedroom mansion in the mountains near Aspen. She had a roof over her head and food to eat. Her bank account wasn't booming, but she wasn't flat broke, thanks to a couple of payments from Simon, a celebrity chef, who'd hired her to edit his latest cookbook. The formerly downward trajectory of her life seemed to have taken a positive turn.

She rose from the chair and she closed *The Legends of Tremont County*, an oversize book with faded sepia photos and an unreliable account of the history for this area. In spite of the outlandish lies and legends, this reading material was dry as a desert before the spring runoff, and that was okay with her. Unlike her dad, Vanessa wasn't looking for adventure.

She went to the tall casement windows in the third-floor library, flipped the latch and cranked one of them open a crack. The early autumn breeze whispered against the glass. She opened the window a bit wider and stuck her head out. The panoramic view was incredible. Late afternoon sunlight spilled across a wide valley. Several miles away was a condo development and in the opposite direction was open range. Once upon a time— over a century ago—this acreage as far as the eye could see belonged to the Whitman family. Her great-great grandfather ran a vast cattle ranch. His son built this massive residence using brick, cedar and chiseled granite, which led to the name Whitman's Castle. Simon owned it now.

He'd inherited the property twelve years ago when his wife, Vanessa's aunt Dorothy, disappeared. Months later, her remains were found, and she was declared dead. There was a legal fuss regarding the terms of her aunt's will, but Vanessa hadn't been living here and hadn't paid much attention. Nor had her father. Dear old Dad—bless his heart—had never been practical when it came to legal matters. She glanced toward the floor-to-ceiling bookshelves where his urn was positioned so she could keep an eye on him.

In her bare feet, she strolled across an exquisite Persian rug. She reached up and lifted the bronze urn from its place of honor. Though she'd searched for the perfect spot to scatter Dad's ashes in the mountains, she couldn't make up her mind. The task had taken on deep significance, and it was important for her to get it right.

Before she moved forward, there were questions from the past that she had to answer. She needed to know where she'd come from before she figured out where she was going. The one good thing about hitting bottom was the chance to start over.

Mona Oliver, the housekeeper, poked her head into the room. A wisp of a woman who almost always dressed in black with a pinstriped apron tied around her waist, she wafted into the library. Her long gray hair was pulled into a tight bun.

As she watched Vanessa place the urn on the library table, Mona clasped her right hand over her heart. "Your father. You miss him, don't you?"

She nodded. "Did you ever meet him?"

"Afraid not. He never came to visit."

"You started working here…when…nine years ago?"

"That's right. Simon had just married Chloe, and she kept me hopping with cleaning, renovation and entertaining." Mona didn't sound unhappy about the extra work. "Busy, busy, busy. The house was full of friends, associates and shirttail relatives, even more than now. Simon loves to play host."

"He's a generous man." Her uncle might be arrogant, hot-tempered and insensitive, but his hospitality was unmatched. "I appreciate what he's done for me."

Mona drifted toward her and lightly touched her arm. "When I mentioned shirttail relatives, I wasn't talking about you, dear. You're not one of those spoiled brats who never make their beds and leave clutter all over. You're tidy. I like that."

"Good, because it looks like I'm going to be staying here awhile longer."

"That's nice, dear. But why?"

"Simon is going to hire me to be his ghost."

Mona's thin eyebrows raised almost to the edge of her widow's peak hairline. "I beg your pardon."

"Ghostwriter," she said with a grin. "He'll

tell me his stories, and I'll put them together in a memoir of his life. After this last cookbook, his publisher asked for a more personal biography embellished with a couple of his favorite recipes."

"I guess that means you'll be an author."

"Not really. I won't have my name on the book."

"Well, that doesn't seem fair. Are you okay with this arrangement?"

"I've always wanted to be a writer." Even though she didn't share her father's gift for poetic language, she enjoyed writing. "Ghosting is a good place to start."

"If you say so." Mona smoothed her apron. "I had a message that there was something you wanted to see me about?"

Vanessa had almost forgotten. "There's going to be one more person for dinner tonight. Sheriff Ty Coleman."

Mona's reaction was unexpected. She fluttered her thin fingers in front of her lips. Her eyebrows danced. And she giggled. "The new sheriff? My, oh, my. Is this a date?"

"I've never met the man. I spoke to him on the phone when I was asking about information in the county files." For the memoir, she needed to find out more about Dorothy's disappearance and death—a sore spot for Simon but significant, nonetheless. "Anyway, I thought it'd be useful to get better acquainted with Sheriff Coleman. You know, for research."

"For your sake, I wish it were a date. You need to start spending time with people your own age. When I say *people*, I mean men."

The housekeeper's matchmaking intentions were clear but irrelevant. Vanessa wasn't looking for a boyfriend. She needed to get herself straightened out before she plunged into a relationship. Still, she promised, "I'll keep my eyes open."

"You won't be disappointed with the view. Sheriff Ty is a pleasure to look at. Did you clear this with Simon?"

"I did."

"So that's an even dozen for dinner," Mona said as she went out the door. "When the sheriff arrives, I'll bring him here to the library so you can meet him, one on one."

"Not necessary," she called after her.

"You'll thank me."

A moment later, Simon made his entrance. He flung his arms wide as if to gather all the energy in the room for his own private use. "I brought the contracts for our writing arrangement. I feel good about working with you, Vanessa, real good. Together, we can heal the family wound."

"Sure."

They'd never discussed the wound, but she knew exactly what he was talking about. Almost twenty years ago when she was ten, there was a rift between Dad and his sister, Dorothy—the estrangement severed their relationship like a machete through butter. Everything changed. Vanessa's parents left Whitman's Castle and moved to Denver. They never made amends, never spoke. Mom died five years later. Then Aunt Dorothy, three years after that.

Like a streak of red lightning, Simon charged across the room toward the long table she used as a desk. He was an outdoorsman, sunburned and ruddy. His dark red hair didn't have a strand of gray even though he was sixty-five. He placed a small stack of legal documents on the table. "I need your signature. Even among family, it's important to have written agreements."

She separated three copies of a five-page contract and sat in her leather swivel chair to study the pages. Earlier, she'd read a draft and needed only to skim. "Give me a minute."

"Let's get a move on. I want to get back to the kitchen to oversee dinner prep." He adjusted the buttons on his chef jacket, which was, of course, deep red.

"You could leave the contracts with me," she said. "I'll give them to you later."

"We'll do it now."

He snapped his fingers at her. Really annoying, but she didn't complain. No point in igniting his firecracker temper. His second wife, Chloe, claimed that his intensity came from being a perfectionist who was overwrought with the responsibilities of the gourmet kitchen in his restaurant, Simplicity. Vanessa didn't think the explanation was that complicated. She believed Simon would be a narcissistic jerk whether he was a chef, car mechanic or surgeon. That was his personality, and she accepted it.

He paced the length of the table, then retraced his steps. His fidgeting distracted her. When she looked up, he was staring. "You know, Vanessa, you look a lot like Dorothy. You have the same honey-colored hair, the same chocolate eyes and the same peaches-and-cream complexion."

His description sounded like a dessert tray. "You've mentioned the resemblance before."

"When you smile, you have the same little gap in your teeth."

While he continued to stare, she flipped through the pages. The document clearly stated a privacy clause that prohibited her from publishing any part of his memoir or research she uncovered without his permission. An understandable concern; he had enemies who would delight in bringing him down.

Her gaze lingered on the amount of her fee, which was broken into thirds. The total was more than she'd make in two years of teaching high school, plus she'd stay here at Whitman's Castle rent-free while she was writing. A very good deal.

She picked up her pen and signed all three copies. Simon did the same. Instead of a handshake, they ended with a hug that he held for two seconds too long. His chef jacket smelled of garlic, grease and a hint of sweat.

"Dinner is at eight," he said. "Eight o'clock sharp."

"I'll be there." She was well aware of his insistence on precision timing for meals, which could be part of his perfectionism or could be a nasty little power trip.

Mona sidled through the door. "Sheriff

Coleman is here. I thought Vanessa could give him a tour of the house before dinner."

When the sheriff stepped inside, Vanessa knew why Mona had hyperventilated at the very thought of this sexy man who was prime boyfriend material. Ty had that cowboy thing going for him—handsome yet unassuming, as though he didn't realize how gorgeous he was. Great body, probably six-four with wide shoulders and narrow hips. He wore jeans and a gray blazer. His dark blond hair was cropped close, military-style. He shook hands with Simon. "Pleased to meet you."

"I can't believe we haven't had you as a guest before. It's wise for those of us in the restaurant business to be friendly with local law enforcement."

"And why is that, sir?"

"Because we're both in the people business. I fill them up, and you take them down. Get it?" Simon brayed a laugh. "How did you and Vanessa meet?"

"Actually, we haven't met," she said. "I spoke to the sheriff when I was looking for documents that might have been filed in the county court."

"Why poke around in that stuff?" Simon's voice took on a darker tone.

"For your memoir. When I talked to your editor, she showed a great deal of interest in the Castle and in Aunt Dorothy."

"Did she?"

Vanessa nodded. Simon himself had mentioned healing the family wound. Why was he angry?

"Let's get this straight, Vanessa. The book is about me. If you have questions about the past, ask me." He turned away from her and spoke to the sheriff. "Have you been to Simplicity?"

"Not yet, but I heard the pepper steak is real tasty."

"Steak au poivre," Simon said. "It's brilliant."

He never missed a chance to lavish praise on his gourmet French/Italian restaurant outside Aspen that was regularly awarded starred Michelin ratings. If she didn't change the subject now, he'd roll through the entire menu. She shook Ty's hand.

The intensity of that casual connection surprised her. A tremor rattled along her spine like a pleasant earthquake. For a moment, she lost herself in the reflection of his gray-green eyes. Struggling to stay on topic, she said, "Maybe you've been to one of my uncle's franchises based on the Simplicity menu. They're called Simple Simon's."

"An unfortunate name," Simon said. "There's nothing simple about me. My partner, Keith Gable, runs the franchise business."

Mona loudly cleared her throat. "Other guests are arriving."

"I suppose I should get back to my ratatouille," Simon said. "Many people don't appreciate the subtleties of the flavor profiles, and—"

"I'm sure they can't wait to try it." Mona the Matchmaker wasn't about to let a recipe stand in the way of what she envisioned as a date. She grabbed Simon's elbow and guided him from the room. "Let's leave these two alone."

Mona closed the door and a wonderful quiet settled around them in the library. The ambient sounds of the household seemed less intrusive. From downstairs, she heard people talking and laughing, preparing dinner. In here, the atmosphere was calm...and safe. How strange to think of safety!

"You haven't been living here long." Ty's baritone hummed with a slight cowboy twang. "Where are you from?"

"I escaped from Denver."

"Escaped?"

She tried to shrug off the word and the implication. The last thing she wanted was to run through the train wreck her life had become. "I might have had a stalker."

"Tell me about him."

"He wore a black ski mask. What a cliché! And he'd follow me around. Once he broke into my apartment and I had to call the police." Her attempt to be nonchalant deflated when she remembered the cemetery. "He tried to attack me."

"What did you do?"

"Threw a Mason jar at him, shot him with pepper spray and ran."

"You did the right thing," Ty said. "If you have any reason to think he's after you again, let me know. It's my job to take care of the people who live in Tremont County."

When he placed a reassuring hand on her forearm, she felt an aftershock of that warm tremor. "Are you ready for the grand tour of Whitman's Castle."

"You bet."

Was he just being polite? A lot of guys couldn't care less about wainscoting, casements and arches. "If you'd prefer, we could go out to the patio for a drink. I've been told that Simon has an amazing collection of wines."

"I'd rather see the house." He shrugged. "Architecture is an interest of mine. I've been a carpenter, off and on, for most of my life."

She could easily imagine him with a tool belt slung around his hips...shirtless and tanned. "Is that what you did before you became sheriff?"

"Mostly, I was a ski bum. In the summer, I worked on carpentry crews. In the winter, ski patrol. After I did some EMT training, I got a job with Search and Rescue. That led to working as a deputy. When the old sheriff died, I inherited his job."

That was a tight little biography. No doubt there was a lot more to say but Ty didn't seem like the kind of guy who bragged about himself. "Why does Mona call you the *new* sheriff?"

"I only got elected a year and a half ago. My job is mostly about handling traffic problems, robberies, bar brawls and domestic fights. I keep meaning to sign up for some forensic classes, but it doesn't seem worth the four-hour drive to a teaching facility. Change comes slowly to the people in

Tremont County. Maybe we're a little old-fashioned. Like this room." He scanned the library. "Looks like it hasn't changed since the early twentieth century. I always wanted floor-to-ceiling shelves, even though I don't have enough books to fill the space."

"Getting the books is easy. Reading them takes more effort." Inwardly, she cringed. What a nerd! "I used to be a high school English teacher."

"I knew you were smart."

She pivoted, grabbed her father's urn off the table and returned it to the bookshelf. Then she marched toward the door. "Come this way."

Somehow, he managed to reach the exit before her and open the door like a gentleman. When she strode through, she felt him following her. His nearness didn't make her nervous. The opposite, in fact. *Safe, I'm finally safe.*

She crossed the wide balcony and spun around to face him. "This forty-five-foot tall room is called the Grand Hall. It separates the original Whitman's Castle from the renovations and additions. The lower part of the opposite wall—" she pointed "—is made of granite mined from a local quarry. The upper part is cedar and was added in 1968."

He leaned over the third-floor railing, gazed to the right, then to the left. "This balcony extends all the way from one end of the hall to the other. I'm guessing about one hundred and fifty feet."

"Close enough. The dimensions on the floor are about the same size as an Olympic swimming pool." She looked up at an arrangement of chandeliers that hung from the ceiling. "Swarovski crystals. That's a one-of-a-kind design, and it's supposed to represent the constellations."

He stared down at the very long dining table in the center of the Grand Hall. Places were already set with china and silverware. "How many people does that seat?"

"Twenty-two, but there are only twelve for dinner tonight."

"I'm impressed."

He sounded surprisingly enthusiastic, and she motioned for him to follow. "At the end of this balcony, there's a staircase that leads down to the second floor where there's another long balcony overlooking the Grand Hall."

On the second floor, she guided him along

the wide balcony, explaining artwork and sculptures she recalled from her childhood. They were about halfway across when a door crashed open and they heard an angry shout. "Listen to me. If they sell, we'll get it all back, every penny. We'll make millions."

Vanessa craned her neck and saw her cousin, Bethany Whitman-Burke, charging in their direction. Her complexion flushed pink under expertly applied makeup, and her long blond hair streamed behind her like a banner. Her black pencil skirt snapped with every stride.

Vanessa managed to leap aside before she got mowed down. "Bethany, are you okay?"

"Shut up, Vanessa. God, you're naive."

She dove into a center room and slammed the door. They heard her fasten the lock, which was very weird. Why would Bethany lock herself in Simon's bedroom?

Chapter Three

Ty stared at the locked bedroom door. Then he looked at Vanessa. Then back at the door. He asked, "What's her name?"

"Bethany Whitman-Burke."

His instincts told him that the blond woman in the tight skirt was a first-degree trouble-maker, but he hadn't come to Whitman's Castle as a law enforcement officer. Supposedly, he was here only as a dinner guest. And he didn't know much about these people. Maybe it was typical for someone to throw a temper tantrum before a formal dinner.

Again, he turned to Vanessa and asked, "Should I talk to her? Do you think she needs help?"

"I don't think so." She shook her head. "The locked door is a fairly serious indication that she doesn't want to be bothered."

"Guess I don't need to bust the door down.

But I've got to ask if Bethany pulls this kind of stunt every night. What can you tell me about her?"

"She's a distant cousin, and I don't know her well. We met for the first time when she and her husband moved in a few weeks ago."

"But you have the same last name."

"There are dozens of people who use the Whitman name and have only a tenuous connection to the family. Mona calls them shirt-tail relatives."

She leaned against one of the vertical posts that supported the balcony and railing. The natural light from the windows at the far end of the Grand Hall had begun to fade, and someone—probably Mona, the house-keeper—had turned on the dangling crystal chandeliers. Pinpoints of light glittered behind Vanessa. In her gauzy blue blouse and denim skirt, she was a vision—a good-looking woman with untamed golden curls, dark eyes and a sprinkle of freckles across her pug nose.

He jerked himself back to reality. "Why do people want to be Whitmans?"

"They think there's an inheritance attached to the name, but they're dead wrong. I'm a direct descendant, and I barely have two nickels to rub together."

Even if that were true, he suspected Vanessa hadn't always been broke. There was something classy about her graceful posture, the way she walked and the way she smiled. Her voice was mellow and precise without being prissy. When she'd invited him to dinner over the phone, he'd been curious to find out more about her, but that wasn't the primary reason he agreed to come to the Castle. A few days ago, he'd gotten a lead on a drug dealer who was working at the Simplicity restaurant, which wasn't the kind of place he could barge into and make demands. He needed finesse. If he had an "in" with Simon, he could learn more about the drugs and arrest the bosses instead of one dumb flunky. More likely, he'd pass his information to the DEA and let them do their job. Ty didn't care about a drug bust; he was happy in his role as the sheriff of a small county where nothing much ever happened.

"What about your family," she asked, "do they live around here?"

"We're from Montana near the Little Bighorn River. When we have reunions, there are dozens of Colemans, and I know every one of them." Family was important to him. Twice every year—at Christmas and in the summer—he returned home to renew, recharge and reassure Ma that marriage and family were still on his horizon. "I have one brother and one sister. You?"

"I'm an only child."

The way she said *only* made him think she was *lonely*, but it was too soon to make that kind of judgment. He stepped up beside her and looked over the edge of the railing. The arrangement of the Grand Hall with two tiers of long balconies seemed appropriate for Simon Markham, who enjoyed looking down on people. Two stories down, Ty saw a platinum blond woman in a white cashmere sweater fussing with the flower arrangements on the long table.

"That's Chloe Markham," Vanessa said.

"I've seen her around town. She almost always wears white."

"That might be why people call her the Ice Princess." Vanessa let her comment dangle, leading him to believe there might be other reasons for the label. "She's quite a contrast with fiery red-haired Simon, but they fit together well. Opposites attract."

He caught a whiff of baked goods and inhaled deeply. "Smells like somebody's baking."

"There's sure to be some kind of bread with the meal."

The thought of fresh-baked bread or muffins—he loved corn muffins—set his belly to rumbling. He hadn't eaten since lunch, and that was only a burger and fries. "How come I smell bread instead of whatever spices go into ratatouille?"

"Blame it on the architecture," she said. "This section of the Castle where we're standing was added to the original structure in 1968. The central part of these three stories and balconies was an interconnected block. On the top floor is the library. The middle—where we're standing—is Simon's master bedroom suite and a guest room with a bathroom. The ground floor is for cooking. When Simon does a big meal, the breads and cakes are prepared in the bakery just off the Grand Hall, and the aroma rises. A delicious anomaly."

"Are the three floor plans similar?"

"There's a dumbwaiter that runs from the top to the bottom," she said. "The placement of windows is the same. Bathrooms are in the same place. And all three floors have a fireplace."

He didn't understand the rationale for constructing the addition in a block but found it interesting. For over a hundred years, Whitman Castle had grown in fits and starts, mimicking the whims of the owners. "Let's see some more of this place."

She led him down a staircase and across the Grand Hall to the original part of the house. The use of chiseled stone and dark-stained wood created an atmosphere suitable for a medieval castle, as did the large proportions of the rooms and the heavy furniture. They crossed a sitting room with glass French doors that opened into an office with a massive desk.

Vanessa was an outstanding tour guide and kept up a narrative of interesting details. In the foyer outside the Grand Hall, she gestured toward a sweeping staircase with carved newel posts. "On the lower level is a movie-screening room with reclining seats and a popcorn machine. Upstairs are more bedrooms, including mine." As she hiked up the staircase, her slender fingers glided along the polished wood bannister. "I probably should have picked a room closer to where I'll be doing my research in the library."

Though the Castle fascinated him, he was equally interested in her. "Research on the book you're writing about Simon?"

"His memoir," she said. "One of the reasons I took on this project was the opportunity to dig into my family's heritage, my roots in Tremont County. I lived here with Mom and Dad until I was ten."

She led the way across the second-floor landing where sliding glass doors opened onto an outdoor deck with a swimming pool and a view of distant peaks. He wouldn't mind waking up every morning to this panorama.

An angular woman who dressed like an old-fashioned librarian stepped through the sliding doors and joined them. Her long gray braid hung halfway down her back. "Sheriff Coleman? Why are you here?"

He heard a tremble of fear in her voice and saw the streaks of tears on her cheeks. "Are you all right, Mrs. Ingram?"

"Fine, I'm fine. It's nice to see you when you aren't wearing your uniform. I mean, you have on other clothes, of course, but you're not so sheriff-like." She twisted her hands in a tortured knot. "You haven't seen my husband, have you?"

"No, ma'am. Are you staying at the Castle tonight?"

A quick nod, and then she said, "I need a drink."

She pivoted, crossed the landing and clomped down the staircase.

Vanessa frowned. "Did she just say that she'd like to see you without clothes?"

"Not exactly."

"How do you know Martha Ingram?"

"Her husband, George, is a retired doctor, and we work together. He's the county coroner. They've lived in these parts for a long time and are as much a part of the community as the yellow gazebo in the town square."

His other connection with them was more personal. He'd arrested their teenaged grandson four or five times, which wasn't information he was free to share with Vanesa.

Time for a change of subject. He pointed to a narrow staircase that led up to another floor. "Where does that go?"

"It's a tower with Aunt Dorothy's sewing room. Simon locked it on the day her remains were discovered and she was declared dead.

As far as I know, nobody has been inside since then."

Ty wasn't surprised to learn that Simon kept his dead wife's room locked and sealed. These people were eccentric. With Vanessa leading the way, they meandered through a labyrinth of twists and turns until he wasn't sure whether they were in the original section or the 1968 addition. On the second floor, they entered a spacious high-ceilinged game room with a pool table, giant-screen TV, game tables, ping-pong and more. Through huge windows that dominated the other distractions, he saw the last rays of sunset.

A skinny man with oversize glasses paced the floor—apparently oblivious to their arrival or anything else. He clenched an unlit pipe in the corner of his mouth.

"That's Bethany's husband," Vanessa whispered. "Lowell Burke. He's a lawyer."

With a start, Burke noticed them. He altered his pacing to aim in their direction. As he came closer, Ty admired his precision grooming. Burke's linen jacket lacked wrinkles, and his jeans had a sharp crease. He removed the pipe, thrust his hand out and offered a quick introduction, including the detail that he and Bethany were from LA and thinking of moving to Colorado.

"We ran into Bethany earlier," Vanessa said.

"Where is she?"

"She ducked into Simon's bedroom and locked the door."

Ty watched Burke for a reaction and saw only a slight furrowing of his brow. "Your wife seemed upset. She said something about millions of dollars."

"There's nothing wrong," he said too quickly. "My wife is a passionate woman. She gets riled up over details."

"What kind of details?" Ty asked.

"Nothing I wish to discuss, Sheriff." Burke's pleasant smile didn't defuse his hostile tone. "Sorry, I'm a bit short-tempered. A misunderstanding with a client. You'll have to excuse me."

Actually, I don't. Ty hadn't been a cop for very long, but he could read Burke's tension and his need to hide his problems. If anything went wrong tonight, Burke would be a suspect. Not that he was here to investigate. "How do you like the mountains?"

"Beautiful." He gestured with his pipe. "Have you seen Keith Gable? I was supposed to meet him here."

"He's probably in the kitchen with Simon," Vanessa said. "You know how those two are all about cooking."

"You're probably right. Bye now."

His speedy exit made Ty think that he was running away from something. Was there a chance that Burke was involved with the drug dealing at Simplicity? The next time Ty talked to the agent he knew at the DEA, he'd suggest checking into the background of Lowell Burke.

"And now," Vanessa said, "here's something most guests don't get to see."

She crossed the room to a row of four pinball machines. The one at the end had a *Star Wars* theme and featured a bright graphic of the princess in a gold bikini. Ty grinned. "My favorite scene."

"Not surprising. All guys love Leia in her gold bra." She paused at the edge of the pinball machine, reached down and twisted a red plastic bar. In response, a section of wall swung open on silent hinges.

He watched as she reached inside and flicked a light switch, illuminating a wrought iron spiral staircase. A secret passageway! He felt like he'd been transported back in time to when he was an eight-year-old kid with a tree house.

"It goes down two stories to the wine cellar," she said.

"We'd better explore."

"You first," she said.

He didn't need a second invite. His boot heels clunked on the metal stairs. The space from one wall to the other was only as wide as the span of his arms. The interior of the secret passage was cedar on the upper part with the staircase firmly bolted in place. When he descended below the first floor, the walls were granite, cool to the touch.

At the bottom of the staircase, she reached over and pulled a dangling chain. A small door swung open, and they were in a basement with rows and rows of wine bottles, properly stored on slanted shelves. He picked up a bottle of dark red burgundy and rolled it around in his hands. A beer drinker, he didn't know much about wine. "Is this a good one?"

"I have no idea." She turned off the light in the secret passage and closed the door.

"When you were a kid, did you sneak through the passage, come down here and steal a bottle of wine?"

"Alcohol didn't interest me, but I loved

being able to disappear into the secret passage. I searched all over the house for another one. There was the dumbwaiter in the library, but it wasn't big enough to hide inside. A couple of the closets have panels in the back where you can hide." She chuckled. "Might come in handy if you're having an affair."

"That makes me think there are a lot of secrets in this house."

"And in this family," she said. "People always talk about the valuable artwork and the worth of the property, but that's not why I love this house. Living here felt like an adventure. It was fun."

"And your family?"

"Well, Simon isn't a real fun guy, but my father was." Her eyes turned misty as she remembered. "John Joseph Whitman was so irresponsible that he drove me crazy, but he could always make me laugh."

He followed her through the rows of wine bottles to a heavy oak door. They both reached for the handle at the same time, and he was glad when their hands touched. Her gaze lifted and she looked up at him. A connection was growing between them. He asked, "Do you have anything else you want to show me?"

"This is enough for one day," she said. "We should go to the patio and have a drink. Dinner is at eight, and Simon is picky about starting on time with all the guests in their assigned seats."

"Sounds like a control freak."

"His house." She shrugged. "His rules."

The flagstone patio behind the house was landscaped with yellow potentilla shrubs and other indigenous flowers and herbs. Fairy lights twinkled on the surrounding pine trees, and Chloe the Ice Princess added her own personal sparkle as she introduced Yuri and Macy Kirov, a well-known couple from Vermont who had been working with Bethany's husband to purchase a local ski lodge. For some reason, Macy—a broad-shouldered, large woman—was dressed like an Amazon with a skimpy outfit, tights with stars and a cape. Ty didn't ask for an explanation, didn't really want to know about her costume.

She gave him a nod and pounced on Vanessa with a voracious grin. "Your father was John. Whitman, right?"

"Yes," Vanessa said.

"I knew him. He was a great skier."

"My wife," Yuri said, "almost qualified for the Olympics."

Ty tapped into a memory from long ago. He'd heard of Macy but her last name wasn't Kirov. "Sanderson, you're Macy Sanderson."

"Good guess, Sheriff. Have we met before?"

"I would have remembered." He recalled a vivid image from a televised downhill race with big, strong Macy dominating the slope. "It's an honor."

Gloria Gable joined them. A former model, she was superchic with thick curly black hair tumbling down her back. Though she'd been married to Keith since before he started the Simple Simon's franchises over ten years ago, she never missed a chance to flirt. She rubbed against Ty's arm like a mountain lioness in heat.

"Sheriff Coleman," she growled in a breathy voice, "I haven't seen you in ages. Miss me?"

"You and your husband," he said. "Where is Keith?"

"In the kitchen with Simon. Of course. The only thing those two get excited about is a new recipe for bouillabaisse."

Keith was another guy he wanted to talk to about the possible drug dealing at Simplicity. Maybe over dinner.

When it was almost 8:00 p.m., Chloe began ushering them toward the Grand Hall. When they were inside, she did a head count. "Where's Bethany?"

She sounded genuinely concerned. Not having the entire crew ready for dinner on time was going to be a big problem. As if he'd been waiting for his cue, Simon marched to the head of the table, greeted his guests and checked his wristwatch.

"There are supposed to be twelve for dinner," he said.

"We're missing Bethany," Mona piped up. "She was upstairs. I'll find her."

Since Ty knew exactly where Bethany was, he fell into step beside Mona. "I'll come with."

"Me, too," Vanessa said.

"Seriously?" Simon barked an angry laugh. "Do we really need three people to find one little blond ditz?"

Vanessa slammed on the brakes. Her fingers pinched into fists. "I thought you might know where she is, Uncle. We saw her run into your bedroom and lock the door."

"My bedroom? What the hell!"

He joined their parade, climbing the staircase at the end of the balcony.

At the locked bedroom door on the second floor, Mona tapped and called Bethany's name. When she got no response, she turned to Ty. "Maybe she doesn't hear me. You can knock louder."

"Sure." He hammered on the door. "Bethany, are you in there?"

Still nothing.

Was there cause for worry? Ty made the transition from polite dinner guest to sheriff. Someone—very likely Bethany—was locked in that room, either afraid or unable to come out. "It's your call, Mona. What should we do?"

"You should kick down the door," she said with an evil little smirk.

"Hell, no," Simon said. "Mona, I'm sure you have a key."

With an annoyed sigh, the housekeeper pulled a huge ring of keys from her pocket and started sorting through them. "You can see why I didn't want to look for the key. This is going to take forever."

"There has to be more than one key," Simon said.

"There are other sets, but they're all the way downstairs in the kitchen."

"Damn it," Simon muttered. He stepped up to the door and pounded on it. "Open up, Bethany. This isn't funny."

Ty couldn't have agreed more. If locking herself in Simon's bedroom had started as a joke—which he doubted very much—the humor was played out. He had a bad feeling about what he'd find behind the locked door.

After an interminable moment, Mona fitted the correct key into the lock. Before anyone could object, Ty moved forward and stood in the open door, blocking access to the bedroom. "I'll take care of this."

"The hell you will." Simon shoved against his chest. "This is my house. Nobody tells me what to do."

"Let's make this easy," Ty said in a low voice. "I won't charge you with obstruction and assaulting an officer, if you step back."

Simon did as he said.

Ty closed the door and locked it behind him. The atmosphere in the master suite felt like empty silence. On the far side of the king-size bed, Bethany was sprawled face-down on the floor. The back of her head was matted and bloody.

Even before Ty failed to find a pulse, he knew she was dead.

Chapter Four

This wasn't the first time Ty was witness to violent death. During the years he worked in Search and Rescue operations, he and his crew had discovered the bodies of rock climbers who fell from great heights and shattered their bones. They found lost hikers, drained of life by hypothermia. Once, they discovered the remains of a man who had been mauled by a mountain lion. A whole family killed in a forest fire. There were occasional hunting accidents, but most of those victims survived. The real danger came when humans pitted themselves against the elements and went one step too far. Nature usually won.

Bethany's death was different. Not an accident. She lay on her belly beside the bed with one arm reaching up and her fingers clutching the silky blue-and-beige spread. She'd been hit at least twice in the back of her skull.

Blunt force trauma; there was a heavy loss of blood. When he leaned down for a closer inspection, he saw white bone shards and brain tissue smeared in her blond hair.

Ty went through the standard procedures, checking for a pulse and shining the light from his cell phone into her eye to see if the pupil constricted. She hadn't been deceased long enough for her body temperature to drop significantly, but her flesh had lost elasticity. Grasped in her fist, he found a gold chain necklace with a locket. The photo inside looked a lot like Vanessa… Curious. He dropped the necklace into the pocket of his blazer, which wasn't protocol but felt like the right move.

If he'd known more about forensics, he might have a better idea of how Bethany was murdered. There were classes on blood spatter that he should have taken, and he could have studied the detailed measurements that showed the amount of force and momentum of the blows. The only conclusions he could draw were obvious. A blood trail on the carpet indicated that she'd dragged herself about ten feet from the center of the room to the bed, maybe trying to reach the telephone on the bedside table. On the floor beside the sofa was a heavy vase, about eighteen inches tall. The white marble base was bloodstained. Murder weapon?

Slowly, Ty stood upright and stepped away from her body. Given the evidence, he knew that Bethany hadn't killed herself.

Her death was a homicide.

And it was his job to find the person who killed her and bring him or her to justice. Clearly, he was going to need help. George Ingram, the local coroner, was out in the Grand Hall, but Ty had seen the old man drinking aperitif wines like water, and wasn't sure how useful the retired doc would be.

Using his cell phone, he connected with Gert, the dispatcher at the station house. Before he could get a word in edgewise, she blurted, "What the heck have you gotten yourself into, Sheriff? I had a call from Mona at Whitman Castle saying something terrible happened. And another call from Special Agent Morris at the Colorado Bureau of Investigation, if you please. I sent you his private number."

"What does the CBI want?"

"No details, but their call was about the Castle. What did you do?"

"Not a damn thing." He knew better than to

give Gert too much information. She wasn't great at keeping secrets. "I can't talk about this, and I don't want you to say anything, either. If anyone asks, just tell them that it's an ongoing investigation."

"Can I say, no comment? I've always wanted to say that. Makes me feel like I'm on the TV."

"Knock yourself out, Gert." This was an all-hands-on-deck situation. All hands meant him and seven officers. "I want you to contact all the deputies and tell them to report to me at the Castle."

"Randall and Chuck have already gone home for the night."

"I need them. As soon as possible."

"You got it, Sheriff."

He ended the call. From outside the closed door, he heard rumblings from the dinner guests who had just become suspects. Someone among them had already contacted the CBI. Probably Simon; he seemed like the sort of guy who always wanted to talk to the person in charge, whether it was the CBI or FBI or the governor himself. Ty didn't much care what the higher-ups had to say. Status wasn't important to him. He'd come to be sheriff as an outgrowth of ski patrol and S&R; his goal actually was to serve and protect the citizens of Tremont County. Never before had he handled a murder.

He glanced toward the door. One of the people out there probably killed Bethany, and he needed to start the investigation. But where? And how? He paced to the door and leaned his forehead against the solid oak. He needed to think. What came first? *The blood.* The killer would likely have blood on his or her clothes. As soon as his deputies arrived, he'd make one of them responsible for checking wardrobes and shoes.

Another deputy would secure the crime scene. No one would be allowed to enter Simon's bedroom until a forensics team recorded the evidence and the body was removed for the autopsy. Those tasks would be passed on to the CBI. Good old Doc Ingram—though he'd been coroner for more than fifteen years—wasn't qualified for postmortem analysis. And as for forensics? Ty mentally scoffed at the idea of a CSI team in Tremont County where taking fingerprints was considered high tech.

Ty ought to speak to Lowell Burke and tell him about his wife's death. But Burke was a suspect. Notification could wait until the deputies arrived and Ty got things under control.

Simon banged on the bedroom door, jolting it. He yelled, "What the hell is going on?"

Ty stepped back. He would have preferred hiding in here until his backup arrived, but he had to face these people and take charge. That was what a sheriff did. That was his job. He straightened his shoulders and emerged from the bedroom onto the wide balcony, closing the door behind him. All conversation stopped. Every eyeball focused on him.

Standing along the balcony were Simon and his wife. His business partner, Keith Gable, leaned against the bannister. Vanessa stood closest to the bedroom door. Her gaze was wary and nervous, though she was the only person who had a solid alibi. She'd been with him the whole time Bethany was locked in the bedroom.

Ty peered over the bannister into the Grand Hall where he saw the doc and his wife sitting at the table, nibbling bread. Burke was deep in conversation with Yuri Kirov. The lawyer didn't seem too concerned about his wife and why she had locked herself in the bedroom. He'd told them that Bethany was a passionate woman. Was that passion a motive for murder? Macy, in her spangled tights, stomped around the table and complained loudly about how hungry she was. Tall, gorgeous Gloria Gable posed with a wineglass in hand and observed the others with the cool disdain of a supermodel.

Simon got up in Ty's face. His complexion was on fire. "What's the deal, Sheriff?"

"Did you call the CBI?"

"I want the best people working on this."

"On what?" Ty met and returned Simon's hostile glare. Did the master of the house know there was a dead woman in his locked bedroom? "What do you think happened?"

"Nothing good, that's for damn sure." He strode toward the closed door and reached for the handle. "Let's find out."

Ty got there first, nudged Simon out of the way and locked the door, which he should have done as soon as he exited. If Simon had charged inside, he would surely compromise the crime scene. "I can't allow you to enter."

"It's my damn house."

Ty wouldn't allow himself to be goaded into an argument. "I appreciate your cooperation. Before you make any more phone calls, consult with me."

Sirens from the police vehicles wailed in

the distance. Ty moved to the bannister and addressed the entire group. "My deputies will be here in just a few minutes. No one will leave the house until we've taken your statements."

"Statements about what?" Simon demanded. "What the hell happened in there?"

"I'm not ready to discuss the situation. Not yet." He turned toward the housekeeper. "Mona, will you tell the kitchen workers and crew that they need to give statements before they go home. Vanessa, come with me."

As he pulled her into the bedroom and closed the door, he realized that bringing her into the crime scene wasn't smart. For all he knew, Vanessa might be the type of woman who puked at the sight of gore or burst into tears. He positioned himself so she couldn't see around him. Bethany's body wasn't visible. "I should have asked before dragging you in here. Are you squeamish?"

"For the past four years, I've been taking care of Dad while he went through every kind of invasive cancer treatment imaginable. It takes a lot to shock me."

"Bethany was murdered."

In spite of her brave words, she cringed. "I'm sorry to hear that."

Her eyes cast downward, and her thick lashes formed crescents on her cheeks. He knew that she wasn't close to Bethany, but the murdered woman was still family. He reached over and patted Vanessa's shoulder. "Are you okay?"

"I guess I'm not as tough as I thought."

"Guess not."

She leaned against his chest. They weren't embracing, but their physical connection seemed to comfort her. She exhaled a sigh. "Is she…is she in here?"

"On the other side of the bed."

She pivoted away from him. "How do you know it was murder?"

"Cause of death was blunt force trauma from severe head wounds. I doubt Bethany could inflict that kind of physical damage on herself."

"Oh, my God, this is terrible. We're lucky that you happened to be here tonight."

He wasn't so sure about that. This investigation felt way out of his depth. He hadn't taken the recommended classes on interrogation, researching suspects and gathering evidence. He wasn't organized. Already, the threads were slipping through his fingers.

"It's my first homicide," he admitted.

"My first time being a suspect." She tried to smile but failed. "That's right, isn't it? I'm on the list."

"You're the only person I'm sure is innocent. We were together the whole time."

"What about the others? The doc and his wife, Macy the skier, Simon himself..." Her voice trailed off. "One of them killed her."

"It's possible there was someone else." But not likely. "Does the Castle have surveillance cameras?"

"It does." She turned to face him. "There must have been a reason you brought me into this room. Why?"

"You impress me as an efficient person, someone who can handle stress."

"Most women would rather hear about their mysterious, stormy eyes or their cascading hair, but efficiency is high praise. I like it. Actually, I prefer it." A slight blush colored her cheeks. He could tell that she was mostly recovered from her initial shock. "How can I help?"

"I need for you to wrangle the guests and employees. Make sure nobody leaves. When my deputies get here, point them in this direction."

"I can handle that." She gave a quick nod.

"Later on, I can help you take statements. I'm all set up for recording in the library."

Somehow, he'd known that he could count on her. "For now, I'll stay here in the bedroom to make sure nobody disturbs the scene."

"Shouldn't be hard." She jabbed her thumb over her shoulder to indicate the door. "That's the only way in or out."

And that door had been locked.

The police sirens were right outside the front entrance. His team had arrived, and he was about to take on a homicide investigation with the kind of locked-room crime scene that baffled great detectives, starting with Edgar Allen Poe. Before he got entangled in the investigation, there was one more thing he wanted to do. He took the necklace from his pocket and held it so she could see. "Bethany was holding this."

"Let me see."

When she reached for the locket, he pulled back. "You should be wearing gloves before you handle evidence."

"So should you."

"I wasn't thinking." He hadn't been pre-pared to deal with a murder, needed to get a grip, stop making mistakes. He opened the locket and showed her the photo inside. "Do you recognize this woman?"

"It's my aunt Dorothy."

"Did Bethany often wear this necklace?"

"I don't think so, but it doesn't look new."

He tucked the necklace back into his pocket. It was evidence, and he had a feeling that it was going to be useful. "If you don't mind, I'd like for you to meet my deputies. Bring Deputy Randall up here and we'll get organized."

"No problem."

As soon as she went out the door, he put through a call to Agent Morris at the CBI. Ty had never met Morris but was familiar with the crisp, official tone of voice. In less than two minutes, he laid out the scanty bit of evidence he had.

"Blunt force trauma," Morris said. "Are you sure she's dead?"

"I'm a trained paramedic. I worked in S&R for five years."

"I know who you are, Ty Coleman. You're the young guy, the former ski bum, who stumbled into a job as sheriff without taking any training or instruction. You don't think you need advice or expertise."

"No, sir, I need all the help I can get."

"You've never reached out before."

"Haven't needed to." Tremont County wasn't exactly a hotbed of criminal activity. Ty and his small department managed to handle the break-ins and drunken brawls and domestic fights without much problem. They had a traveling judge who opened the courtroom for a few hours on Tuesdays and Thursdays. Their small, sparsely populated county should have allowed itself to be absorbed into neighboring Pitkin County, but a long-ago feud kept them separate.

"What's your angle?" Morris asked.

"Don't have one."

"Because of Simon Markham, the Castle and Macy Kirov the competitive skier, this murder is going to be high-profile. This investigation might be something that would boost the career of a sheriff in a small mountain county."

Ty ignored the hint. He hadn't sought this position and wasn't a political animal. "I'll say it again, Morris. I need your help. I need your forensic team to process the crime scene. And your computer experts. And I want to hand over the body. Our county coroner doesn't do autopsies."

"Sounds to me like you want the CBI to do all your work."

"Your people know what they're doing. They have experience. We haven't had an actual murder investigation in Tremont County in years."

"Are you willing to cede jurisdiction?"

"In a heartbeat," Ty said. "This is your case and welcome to it."

"I have an agent in Aspen. He'll be in touch within the hour."

"I'll be waiting for his call." Ty couldn't wait to drop this ticking time bomb into somebody else's lap.

Chapter Five

An hour later, Vanessa sat at the long table in the library, waiting to interview her first suspect. Outside, the night had become turbulent. A fierce wind howled past the windows.

Glad to have something to keep her busy, she looked down at the notebook in front of her. Several of her to-do items had already been crossed off. Though this was the first homicide-investigation list she'd ever made, the organizational principles were the same as a housework list or a work project. She started by jotting down the primary goal, which, in this case, was interview suspects. Then she itemized her needs for the project, including pens, paper, recording equipment and drinking water. Then she listed the dinner guests.

Ty had been right about her. One of her best talents was efficiency. Working together, they'd already delegated several tasks to his deputies. One stayed at the crime scene and took photos on his cell phone. Another checked for traces of blood on clothes and in the guests' bedrooms. Fingerprinting and collecting DNA evidence would wait until the CBI agents arrived with forensic teams.

One of the deputies escorted Keith Gable into the library. She gave him a friendly wave and said, "Keith, would you please take a seat?"

"Why?"

"I'm doing preliminary interviews for the police. I need to record your name, address and approximate whereabouts at the time of Bethany's murder."

A few days ago, she'd set up an area in the library where she could talk to Simon and record his recollections for the memoir. The arrangement was perfect for suspect interviews.

"Am I the first?" he asked.

"You are."

She didn't know him well, even though they'd both lived at the Castle off and on. Keith's primary offices for the Simple Simon's franchise restaurants was in Denver, and she'd considered going to work for him after she finished ghosting Simon's memoir. Not that he'd invited her.

Self-interest was Keith's trademark. If she'd had something he wanted, he'd be all over her. Otherwise…nothing. He was an average-looking guy with a million-watt smile—a talented salesman who convinced the patrons of Simple Simon's that a common hot dog was a gourmet treat. He perched on the edge of the chair opposite her, leaned forward, rested his elbow on the table and shaded his eyes as though the light was too bright. "Let's get rolling, Vanessa."

As if he has somewhere else to be? "I assume our addresses and phone numbers for you are correct."

"Of course."

"Where were you tonight between six thirty and eight?"

"In the kitchen. I was trying to convince Simon to add croquettes to the Simple Simon's menu—chicken, crab and veggie."

"Crab?" She was surprised by the addition of an expensive item.

"Imitation crab. Do you think I want to go broke?"

She'd think that he'd want to serve his patrons the best crab croquette possible, but didn't press the point. "During that hour and a half, did you ever leave the kitchen?"

"I suppose I had a bathroom break."

She remembered the conversation she and Ty had with Bethany's husband. "Lowell Burke was looking for you. Did you find each other?"

He tilted back in his chair, focused on her and flashed the sparkling smile. "Why are you working with the police, Vanessa?"

"The sheriff needed some help."

"Sheriff Ty Coleman," he said. His smile grew broad and seductive. "I noticed that you changed into skinny jeans and a low-cut T-shirt. Very sexy. Are you dating Sheriff Ty?"

"I just met the man tonight, and the atmosphere hasn't exactly been romantic, what with the blunt force trauma and all."

"So that's how Bethany died. Somebody beat her over the head. Did you see the body? Can you tell me anything else?"

Vanessa dropped an embarrassed glance at the recorder that was taking down every word of her lapse in judgment. She shouldn't have said anything about the murder, shouldn't have allowed Keith to manipulate their conversation.

"Bethany's husband," she said. "Did you see him?"

"I did, and we agreed to talk later."

"Other than the bathroom break, did you leave the kitchen?"

"I checked on the breads in the Grand Hall baking area. And I went into the employee locker room to get a clean jacket." He smoothed the front of his pristine white chef coat. "Some idiot pastry chef slopped cherry compote on me."

"How long were you gone on each of these occasions?"

"Come on, Vanessa. You can't really think that I hurt Bethany. Especially not by bludgeoning. I'm a chef. Obviously, my murder weapon of choice would be poison."

"What are you telling me?"

Abruptly, he stood. "We're done here."

She agreed. Her job wasn't to interrogate him. All she needed was a statement of his alibi to give the real detectives a starting point. She followed Keith to the library door. When he exited, Martha Ingram and Ty entered. Martha flew into Vanessa's arms and wrapped her in a tight hug. The gray-haired lady was so skinny that Vanessa could count every rib.

"My dear, dear, dear young lady," Martha said, "I'm so very sorry about your cousin's death. You must be devastated."

Devastated was a strong word and not altogether appropriate. Though unhappy about Bethany's murder, Vanessa wasn't deeply affected. She expected the husband to handle the funeral arrangements and such. Still, she agreed with Martha. "It's a terrible thing."

"To think, she's still up in that room. The police haven't removed her body. That is downright disrespectful." She exhaled in a huff, and Vanessa caught a strong whiff of whiskey on her breath. Martha stared at Ty. "Can't you do something about poor sad Bethany?"

"It's okay, Mrs. Ingram. Everything is under control." He took her elbow, guided her to the library table and seated her in the chair Keith had vacated. "Vanessa is going to ask you a few questions. Just answer as best you can."

Talking to Martha should have been easy, but she'd been drinking and seemed upset. Vanessa wasn't sure she could handle the woman. She looked to Ty. "Maybe you should do this interview."

"You'll do fine." His phone pinged, indicating a new text message, and he crossed the library to stand in front of the fireplace while he read it and answered.

Martha Ingram composed herself. Her bony fingers laced in a knot on the tabletop. "Go ahead, dear."

"Does Chloe have your correct address and phone number?"

"I'm sure she does. George and I haven't moved or changed the number in twenty years. It was always our dream to retire to the mountains. Back then, we were both avid skiers."

Vanessa listened politely while Martha launched into a monologue about how skiing had gotten too expensive and the crowds were too big loud and aggressive. The longer she talked, the more heated her language became, leading to a pattern of curse, apologize, curse, apologize, then curse, curse, curse. She had a weird habit of playing with her long gray braid, pulling it over one shoulder and then the other. Bright spots of color appeared on her cheeks.

"Are you all right, Martha?" Vanessa reached for the glass pitcher on the table. "Should I pour you a glass of water?"

"Yes, damn it. Oh, I'm sorry. Damn, damn, damn."

"Only one more question," Vanessa said. "Where were you between six thirty and eight?"

"I don't know."

This interview was a disaster. "Do you remember when Sheriff Coleman and I saw you earlier tonight? We were near the swimming pool."

"Yes," she said brightly. "I was looking for George."

"Where were you before that?"

"In our bedroom, taking a nap."

"And after?"

Martha's forehead scrunched. "I wandered downstairs. The Castle is so big that I tend to get lost and wander. But I heard voices."

"You said you wanted a drink," Vanessa prompted.

"Now I recall." She snapped her fingers. "I went outside to the patio, found George and got a Manhattan from the bartender."

"Good job, Martha. That's all I need to know."

When Ty joined them at the table and patted the older woman's scrawny arm, Martha calmed. She gazed warmly at the sheriff, flipped her braid and lowered her voice to a whisper. "I shouldn't speak ill of the dead. It's not right but might be something you need to know."

"It's okay, Mrs. Ingram," he assured her. "You don't have to tell us anything else. This is just a preliminary interview. Tomorrow, the agents from the Colorado Bureau of Investigation will go into detail."

"Well, I'm certainly not going to talk to those Denver people—those flatlanders." She stiffened her spine and lifted her chin. "I don't want them poking around in my business."

"What business is that?"

"I don't care about rumors, don't care about what people are saying. My husband is a good man. George would never be disloyal to me."

Vanessa remembered that when they first saw Martha, she looked like she'd been crying. Did she actually suspect her husband of having an affair? The man had to be in his seventies. "I'm sure he's faithful, Martha. How long have you been married? Thirty-five or forty years?"

"He doesn't look like a philanderer." She quietly cursed. "For your information, dear, my George is a silver fox. There's snow on the roof, but he's got a fire in his belly."

Vanessa wasn't about to argue with that statement. She nodded. "Okay."

"I'm his second wife, you know. Fifteen years younger than George, and I was quite a beauty when we hooked up. I was blond like Bethany." She bolted to her feet, cursed and apologized. "Everybody in town knows that she's been having an affair."

Ty stood beside her. He didn't have an expressive face, but she could tell that he was surprised by Martha's statement. He cleared his throat. "Who told you about the affair?"

"I don't remember. Somebody in the diner or at the church."

"And did they tell you it was George?"

"Absolutely not. Nobody knows the name of her lover, but you can bet your booties that he's married and a big fat cheater."

"Thanks for the information, Mrs. Ingram." He guided her toward the door. "I'm going to have Deputy Randall escort you to your room. I want you to go to bed and get a good night's sleep. We'll talk again tomorrow."

As soon as the door closed behind her, Ty leaned his back against it and exhaled in a whoosh. His shoulders sagged. "That was a whole lot more than I wanted to hear."

"But it's important. If Bethany was having an affair, that gives people a reason to want her dead."

"A motive," he said. "But can we believe what Mrs. Ingram said?"

"We can't ignore it."

He shrugged. "We'll pass on the recordings to the CBI."

She didn't understand his reluctance. Not that she was a detective, but Vanessa had seen enough movies and read enough books to know that motive was vital to crime solving. Ty ought to be formulating plans to dig deeply into Bethany's possible indiscretions. "We need to check this out," she said. "Maybe she was killed by her lover to protect his reputation."

"Or by his wife to save her marriage."

"His wife?" When Vanessa visualized murder by clubbing someone over the head, she thought of brute force. "Would a woman have the strength?"

"Macy Kirov is a big strong woman—a former professional skier." Ty stepped away from the door and paced into the center of the library. "Gloria Gable works out every day to keep that sleek supermodel figure. Chloe Markham is in good shape."

His logic encouraged her. She could tell that he'd been thinking about suspects. "You should stay with me while I finish these interviews. These people are more comfortable with you. They'll open up."

"I'm not in charge. The murder isn't my jurisdiction."

"But you're the sheriff, and the Castle sits in the middle of Tremont County."

"I ceded authority to Agent Morris of the CBI. He's in charge, and he already sent over a team from Aspen to remove the body, take fingerprints and DNA samples."

"That cop from Aspen. What was his name? Jenkins?"

"His name is Jack." Ty approached her, placed his hands on her shoulders and gazed into her eyes. "We have to cooperate with these guys. They're experienced. They've got the tools and know how to use them."

Their physical connection felt warm and secure, calming and exciting at the same time. Her natural inclination was to glide her hands around his torso and pull him toward her until they made full body contact and melted against each other. Inappropriate? Totally!

She tossed her head and forced a smile. "I'll get back to my interviews."

"Not a good idea," he said. "I shouldn't have given you this assignment in the first place. You're not a cop. I shouldn't have put you in danger."

"But I'm fine, and I want to be involved."

"When you told me about your stalker back

in Denver, I advised you to report that kind of danger to me. I'm a sheriff. It's my job to protect you."

Though she liked the idea of Ty being her protector, Vanessa was far from helpless. "I haven't been threatened."

"You can't ignore facts, Vanessa. Someone in this house is a murderer."

She was aware of the probability that the person who killed Bethany was one of the dinner guests. But they had no motive to come after her. She liked being involved in the investigation and despised the idea of sitting around, doing nothing and twiddling her thumbs. "I'll be fine."

"Your next interview is with the most likely suspect."

She thought for a moment. "I know who that is."

"Tell me."

"If Bethany was having an affair, the man with the strongest motive for revenge is her husband. Plus, the police always look to the spouse. It's Lowell Burke."

"And I should keep an eye on him." Ty poured himself a glass of water from the pitcher on the table. "I'll stay."

Chapter Six

Water glass in hand, Ty paced around the perimeter of the library, which he had decided was his favorite place in the Castle—not the swimming pool or the secret passage, not the game room, certainly not the tragic bedroom on the floor below where Bethany had been murdered. Vanessa's library had a warm, cozy feeling, probably because she spent time here and the library reflected her personality: organized, quiet and comfortable.

He paused at the end of the table that was opposite from where Vanessa had her recording equipment. Outside the three tall casement windows, a fierce wind tossed the pine branches like a typhoon churning in troubled seas. Nature was giving him a warning. .

Every person in the house was a suspect. Worse, they were all in danger from the killer. Vanessa's position was the most precarious because she was the only guest with a private bedroom. If the killer attacked, she had nowhere to hide, no one to help. Before he left tonight, he'd make sure she was safely locked in her room.

Lowell Burke entered the library. Ty tried to work up a decent amount of empathy for the recently widowed man but couldn't get past his prissy attitude or his narcissism.

An hour ago, when Ty had informed Burke that his wife was dead, the well-dressed lawyer reacted with a credible display of shock. His knees folded, he collapsed into a chair and slouched over, holding his head in his hands. His cheeks were wet with tears. When he wiped his face with a tissue, it was obvious that Burke was wearing makeup—a trend Ty hoped wouldn't catch on. A lot of men wanted to look like they'd just come from the golf course or from schussing down the slopes on a perfect spring day, but they didn't take part in sports. Instead, they used spray tans or foundation makeup.

Burke had taken the time to repair his mottled cheeks, creating a smooth mask that wasn't fooling anybody. His level of tension was through the roof. If twisted one notch higher, the nervous lawyer might explode.

He'd changed his shirt and trousers. Ty made a mental note to have one of his deputies locate the clothes Burke had been wearing earlier and check for bloodstains.

Burke asked, "What's this about, Sheriff?"

"Just a quick interview to gather name, address and phone numbers. Tomorrow, Agent Morris of the CBI will take over. Vanessa and I are just getting the preliminaries out of the way." Ty paused for a moment, watching Burke for his reaction. "There's no need for you to call your lawyer. Not yet, anyway."

"Are you implying that I'm a suspect?"

Too subtle? "I'm not implying anything."

"Go to hell, Sheriff." He pivoted and took a step toward the door. "I'll talk to the *real* detectives tomorrow."

"Oh, please," Vanessa said. "Sit down, Burke. At least you can allow me to verify your name and address."

He pushed his glasses up on his nose. "Why should I?"

"Because you want to do anything to help find Bethany's killer. Otherwise—" she paused for effect "—it looks bad."

Since he couldn't argue with that, he dropped into the chair beside her and crumpled like a painted marionette with cut strings. He whined. "Nobody understands how hard it is to lose a beloved spouse. How will I go on?"

Ty sipped his water and said nothing while Vanessa comforted and consoled. She even called down to the kitchen to request a fresh-brewed cup of chamomile tea for the grieving husband. When she started with her questions, Burke stretched every response into an essay. He couldn't say what his address was because he and Bethany had lost their house in LA and were having mail forwarded to the Castle. Did she want his post office box? The one in LA? The one in Aspen?

Finally, Vanessa got to the meat of the interview. "Where were you between six thirty and eight?"

"My alibi?" Burke shot a hostile glance at Ty. "Waiting in the game room to meet Keith. That was where the two of you found me and suggested that I look for him in the kitchen, which was exactly what I did. We had a brief chat. You can verify with Keith. Then I went outside to the patio where I talked with Chloe and Gloria. And, of course, Macy and Yuri, my clients."

"If you don't mind my asking," Vanessa

said, "what kind of work are you doing for Macy and Yuri Kirov?"

"Real estate, which is my specialty. They want to buy Simplicity and a few other properties in the area."

"That must be complicated work," she said. "Was that transaction the reason Bethany was so riled up and talking about millions of dollars?"

"She had everything tangled with Aunt Dorothy's death and her estate. That story is ancient history based on gossip and fantasy. There are no missing millions."

"And she thought she was due an inheritance," Vanessa said. "Why?"

"Bethany never explained herself in rational detail." His voice softened. "I was the sensible partner, and she was the dreamer."

"Are you certain that she didn't know anything?"

"She was obsessed."

"As a lawyer, you don't need to believe in a fairy-tale payoff," Vanessa said. "Your commission on the sale of Simplicity ought to be substantial."

"And I will have earned every penny with my skill and expertise."

"There's nothing like an honest day's work."

Ty grinned at Vanessa. He'd heard the sarcasm in her tone—a nuance that flew over Burke's head. It was amazing that the shifty lawyer actually thought his manipulations and documents equated with *real* work.

One of the guys from the kitchen came into the library with a tray holding a steaming mug of tea. Burke stood and made a twirling motion with his index finger to indicate that the man with the tray should turn around. "We're done here, right?"

"I believe so," Vanessa said.

After the door closed behind Burke, Ty scooted down the table and sat beside her as she pressed Stop on the recording. "Good interview, lady. I especially like the way you managed to talk to him without giving him a smack on the jaw when he meandered off the topic. You're very patient."

"I've had plenty of practice listening to Simon's stories for his memoir. He and Burke are both egomaniacs."

"Narcissists," he said.

"I also taught high school English for four years, which gave me experience in dealing with the adolescent mind."

Ty stuck his hand into the pocket of his blazer and wound the gold chain around his fingers. He shouldn't be touching the necklace. This was evidence, but he glided his thumb over the etched design on the front of the locket—a heart with an arrow that circled it.

He should have checked for prints as soon as he took the necklace from Bethany's hand. Too late now. "From what Burke said, Bethany was obsessed with Aunt Dorothy."

"Much as I hate to agree with Burke, I think he's right about the many variations on the Dorothy story. It's based on rumor and fantasy."

"Tell me about her disappearance."

"I don't know much. My family—Dad, Mom and I—were estranged from Dorothy and Simon twenty years ago. Five years later, Mom died. After that, my father spent all his time traveling, writing poetry, teaching a college seminar and ignoring all things Whitman. Twelve years ago, Dorothy went out for a ride on her horse and never returned."

"How old were you?" he asked.

"A freshman in college at Northwestern in Chicago. I'm ashamed to admit that I didn't come back for the memorial service."

"You said she disappeared. Was her body found?"

"There were many days of searching. It was the beginning of winter and a blizzard made it impossible to continue the search. After the spring thaw, her remains were found. Doc Ingram declared her dead."

"George Ingram?" Ty shouldn't have been surprised to hear the coroner's name. "Are we talking about the silver fox?"

She nodded. "Apparently, they discovered enough of her remains to make a DNA identification."

"No signs of foul play?"

Her eyebrows lifted. "None that I know of. I like this change in attitude. You sound like a detective."

"I am, in fact, the sheriff of this county." He didn't have training in forensics or profiling or cyber investigation, but he had sworn an oath to take care of the over twelve thousand residents of Tremont County. If that meant calling upon experts, he'd do it. If there were pieces of this murder that he could solve himself, Ty was ready. "I'm asking again. Any reason to believe that Aunt Dorothy was murdered?"

"From what I've heard, that's where the

rumors kick in." She stood behind the table, rolled her shoulders and flexed her arms. "Some people blamed Simon for Dorothy's disappearance, which they said was an accident that could have been avoided if he'd gone with her on her ride or initiated the search earlier. Others called it a tragic mishap when she was thrown from her horse, suffered a concussion and died. Most people believed that the local scavengers pulled her body apart. On the opposite end of the spectrum, there were people who believed Dorothy was murdered."

"By her husband?"

"Simon would be the logical suspect." She stretched again and yawned. "The money he inherited from Dorothy's estate, including property and possessions, was enough to refinance Simplicity and to start up the Simple Simon's franchises."

All those pieces added up to a ton of motive. Ty watched as she went to the tall window and rested her slender fingers against the pane as though she could reach through the transparent glass and touch the wind. Her mood was pensive and magical. "You don't think Simon killed her."

"If I believed he was a murderer, I couldn't

work for him." She spun around and faced him. "Simon is an irritating person. Like you said, a narcissist. But he loved Dorothy. My father didn't care for either of them, but he respected their relationship, and he wasn't surprised when he heard that Simon had sealed off Dorothy's sewing room. That's the act of a desperate and heartbroken man."

She believed the words she was saying. Ty heard the ring of steel in her voice and saw a flash of determination in her eyes. "Have you spoken to your uncle about Dorothy's death?"

"Not yet, but it's a conversation we'll need to have. The editor who is going to publish his book already mentioned that she was interested in more than Simon. She wants details about Dorothy's tragic death and photos of the Castle."

He suspected the murder of Bethany would hype interest in the house, and he wondered who would benefit from that publicity. "Why is she interested in the Castle?"

"It makes Simon unique. Instead of the standard backstory about learning how to boil pasta at his grandma's knee, he can be portrayed as the chef who recovered from losing his adored wife and built a cooking empire from a castle."

"When you start digging, be prepared for what you might find."

"I planned to start with court records."

"That's why you contacted me." He would have been willing to help without being offered a dinner at the Castle. Now that he'd met Vanessa, Ty would happily spend hours researching with her. "There are a lot of people with information, starting with Doc Ingram."

"And Keith was involved in building the franchises. He knew Aunt Dorothy."

"I could get you an interview with the Search and Rescue teams," he offered. "I'd like to hear their explanation about why it was so hard to find her remains."

"I need to be careful about releasing too much information. My contract with Simon has a nondisclosure clause." After one last stretch, she returned to her seat at the table and pressed the button that signaled she was ready to continue. "Here we go. Send in the clowns."

"All that yawning. Are you tired?"

"Not really."

He still had concerns about her safety. "Be careful, Vanessa. When you're done here, hit my phone number on your speed dial and I'll walk you to your bedroom."

"I'll give you a buzz."

The door crashed open, and Macy Kirov stalked inside. Her tights sparkled, and her cape swirled behind her. In her left hand, she held a plate of macadamia nut cookies and fudge. "Anybody hungry?"

"You bet." Ty grabbed one of each as he exited.

VANESSA FINISHED HER interviews just before midnight. She was exhausted and achy from the tension that tied the muscles across her shoulders into tight little knots. With a prolonged groan, she forced her legs to stand, then she staggered across the room to the long leather sofa under a huge painting of snow-capped peaks and a frozen creek winding through a forest. She collapsed and groaned again. Though she could have fallen asleep in about two minutes, she'd promiscd Ty that she'd call when she was done. She punched his number on her speed dial.

He answered after the second ring. "Finished with the interviews?"

"I am, and I didn't learn anything new, other than Macy would happily slaughter any woman who had an affair with her husband. Her exact words were *nobody touches my Yuri.* Which sounds a little bit dirty."

He chuckled. "You're funny."

"Yeah, I'm a hoot." Although she appreciated the compliment, Vanessa would have preferred a comment about her lovely smile or gorgeous figure. Why had Keith been impressed by the sexy fit of her skinny jeans while Ty barely noticed she was female? She'd always had admirers when it came to her brainpower. Her sexiness? Not so much. "I also discovered that Gloria Gable bench presses ninety-five pounds and certainly has the upper body strength for blunt force trauma. Simon and Chloe are both furious about a murder happening in their Castle."

"Where are you?" he asked.

"Still in the library."

"I had to go out to my car and pick up a few things. I'm headed back to the house. If you want, you can wait for me in the library. Or you can have the deputy who has been outside your library door all night escort you to your bedroom."

Or I can walk there all by myself. "I'm tired. I'll grab the deputy."

"And I'll check in with you."

She stood, straightened her shoulders and

opened the library door. Deputy Randall was
waiting. Dressed in his black uniform shirt
with his badge and utility belt, he looked
every inch a cop, but his grin was shy and
his attitude friendly. When she thanked him
for staying here tonight and asked about his
kids, he was happy to chat about his four-
year-old daughter.

Down the stairs and across the Grand Hall
and up the stairs again, Randall regaled her
with one story after another. All Vanessa
could think about was getting to her bedroom
and sleeping. At the door to her second-floor
bedroom, he touched the brim of his cowboy
hat and bid her good-night. "Don't forget to
lock up," he warned.

It took willpower to keep from flopping
down on her cozy double bed with the hand-
made quilt in shades of green and blue. Vanessa peeled off her clothes and changed into
a pair of silky black pajamas. As soon as she
threw back the quilt and slipped between the
sheets, her brain started running at top speed.
The faces of the suspects flashed before her.
Each looked more guilty than the one before.
Then she thought of Bethany.

They hadn't been close, but Vanessa would
miss her cousin. Was she killed because of

an affair? What a sad, stupid reason! Or was the motive something else, something associated with the disappearance of Aunt Dorothy?

Eyes wide open, Vanessa stared up at the bedroom ceiling. Moonlight poured through the window, and a sudden gust rattled the glass in the frame. The cry of the wind sounded like a tortured voice in mourning. Then she heard it. "Vanessa, Vanessa, I won't hurt you, Vanessa."

She bolted from the bed. The words were the same, but that voice couldn't be her stalker. She was overtired. Her imagination was getting the best of her.

"Vanessa," he hissed. "Go to the window. Look to the Hag."

Where are you? He wasn't in her bedroom, but his voice was close. There must be a recording hidden in here or a remote-activated microphone.

She went to the window. Her bedroom was on the second floor, too high for the stalker to reach her, and she had locked the door.

Peering into the night, she watched the wild dancing of wind-swept tree branches. Across a shallow ravine was a massive rock formation called the Hag Stone because the profile looked like an old witch hunched over her cane. When she was a kid, she had imagined the giant hag coming to life and stalking toward the Castle.

Halfway up the stone on an outthrust ledge, she saw him. A man dressed all in black, wearing a ski mask. Her stalker. He raised his arm and pointed at her.

Chapter Seven

Panic overwhelmed her. Vanessa stopped breathing. She blinked several times…nearly lost consciousness. It felt like the world had stopped spinning. *This can't be happening.* When she opened her eyes and looked around, she was all the way across the room from the window, pressed up against the edge of her desk and unable to breathe. *It can't be him.* She hadn't seen any sign of the stalker since she drove away from the Denver cemetery with Dad's ashes in the passenger seat. Why would he appear now? *Oh, God, what if he was the murderer?*

She covered her face with her hands. Was she imagining the man in black? Was he her personal bogeyman who appeared when she was scared or angry? She returned to the window and peered into the windy night. Tree branches dipped and waved. Small puffs of clouds scudded across the sky like whitecaps on a blustery sea. The Hag Stone loomed before her. It almost looked like the Hag was moving with the shadows dashing across the rocks.

Her stalker had vanished. She saw no sign that he'd been standing there, pointing at her in a silent threat. She listened to the shrieking wind and didn't hear anything resembling words. No one called her name or poisoned her mind with false statements about not wanting to hurt her. But she knew he was out there. When he'd appeared at the cemetery, she ran away. *Not this time.*

Vanessa wouldn't flee from him. Nor would she cower behind a locked door in her bedroom. She had to find this guy and figure out what he was after.

Before she could reconsider, she thrust her feet into sneakers and covered her pajama top with a denim jacket. In the back of her underwear drawer, she found a small flashlight. Her canister of pepper spray was also in there, but she decided she wouldn't need it. This time, she wouldn't confront her stalker alone. She had Ty on her side.

He'd promised to check in, but she couldn't wait for him. She needed to run to the Hag

Stone and find that creep before he had time to escape. One of the other deputies stationed in the Castle could accompany her.

She grabbed her phone and keys, and stepped into the dimly lit hallway with lantern-style sconces and framed pictures commemorating the many trips her family had taken. There was a Grand Canyon photo of Vanessa as a gangly eight-year-old with pigtails. She was surrounded by Dad and Mom and Aunt Dorothy. The older generation was gone. This was the end of an era.

Holding her phone to call Ty, she rushed down the corridor. On the landing at the top of the staircase, she saw a tall cop in a black uniform shirt, weathered leather jacket and a cowboy hat. Was he a sheriff? Was he a cowboy? Both! "Ty?"

"I'm here."

His presence calmed her panic and refreshed her mind. Ty Coleman was the perfect adversary for her bogeyman. He'd kick her stalker's rump.

Without thinking, she threw her arms around him. His body was as hard and muscular as she had imagined. He smelled like soap, even though she knew he hadn't had time for a shower. Her hands slid down his torso to the holster on his utility belt. "Oh, good," she said. "You have a gun."

"What's going on, Vanessa?"

"He's here. The creep who was stalking me in Denver is here."

"Did you see him?"

She nodded vigorously. "I looked out my window toward the Hag Stone. The wind was blowing, and the tree branches were waving frantically, like fans at a Broncos game. First, I heard his voice, calling my name. Then I saw him standing on a ledge on the Hag. I turned away, and when I looked back, he had disappeared."

Ty kept one strong arm around her and smoothed the hair off her temple with his other hand. "Let me take care of this."

"No," she said emphatically. "I'm not going to hide in my room, and I won't run away. We—that's you and me—have to go after the stalker right now. Together."

"Or I can call Deputy Randall to stay with you. I'll search outside."

"How will you know where to look?"

"I'll figure it out."

She was skeptical…and insulted. He didn't seem to be taking her seriously. She pushed away from him, stepped back and studied his expression. "You don't believe me."

"I didn't say that."

He didn't have to be direct; she'd heard the tinny note of condescension in his voice. He was humoring her. "I'm not hallucinating. This isn't an anxiety attack or a post-traumatic stress episode. I'm going downstairs and out the door. I'll find him and bring him back."

"All by yourself?"

"If necessary." She stuck out her chin. "I'd prefer having you with me because I don't know how dangerous this guy is. And you have a gun."

Ty wasn't the kind of man who wasted time on discussion. He took off his cowboy hat, ran his hand through his short-cropped hair and replaced the hat. "Let's go."

Downstairs, she led him to an exit that went through a mudroom attached to the kitchen. After she inserted a plastic card and pressed five numbers on a keypad, the lock clicked open.

"How does that work?" he asked. "Does the code change every day?"

"It's kind of like an ATM. We all have our own code." This door wasn't the most direct route to the Hag Stone, but it was an exit she had access to. "Didn't Simon explain all this when he showed you the feed from the security cameras?"

"We didn't get that far. Simon wanted to wait for Special Agent Morris before he shared his secrets."

"That must have ticked you off."

"Yeah, it did. I assigned one of my deputies to watch the security feeds."

"And that must have made Simon angry."

"I'm the law. I make the rules."

In his uniform, he looked more authoritative than when he was wearing a sports jacket. "Where did you get your outfit?"

"My car," he said. "I don't have much hope in finding an intruder on the security cameras. In a house big enough to be called the Castle, there's no way to monitor every person who enters or exits. An intruder could slip in an open window or a secret passage."

She stepped outside. Though there was a lull in the wind, she dug into a pocket of her jacket and pulled out a woolen headband with a Norwegian pattern. She wrapped it across her forehead and over her ears. Then she took out her flashlight but didn't turn it on. There was enough moonlight to see where they were headed.

Through a clearing and beyond a couple of outbuildings, she found the path that ascended the rocky forested hillside. When they were directly above the horse barn, she made a steep right turn and went higher.

"You were right," he said. "I needed you to show me the way. I never would have found this path by myself."

"I don't believe that for a minute," she said. "Do you hunt? I'm guessing you can track a bunny rabbit on a rainy day."

"Good guess, except I don't hunt bunnies. I learned most of my tracking skills with Search and Rescue."

He was a man with many useful talents. "There are several ways to get to the Hag Stone, but this is the most direct. No caves, but many good hiding places."

"How do you know all this?"

"I've had time to climb around on the rocks. Ever since I got here, I've been looking for the perfect place to scatter Dad's ashes."

"The urn in the library?"

"Yes." She hadn't meant to get sidetracked by mentioning her father's death and rapidly changed the subject. "We need to be prepared for the stalker. He could be hiding anywhere."

Ty drew his Glock and pulled a high-power Maglite from one of the compartments on his utility belt. On the dark side of the cliff, he aimed the flashlight to show obstacles along the narrow uneven trail. In the dark, it was hard not to stumble. She wanted to dash up the hillside. Her anxiety urged her to move faster. But she didn't want to fall.

"Up there," she said as she pointed to the outcropping of rock. From this angle, the shape didn't resemble an old witch bent over her cane. "Do you see that ledge? That's where he was standing. He took a threatening pose, exactly the way he did in Denver."

Ty hunkered down beside a clump of chokecherry bushes, most of which hadn't lost their leaves. "Access to the ledge looks tricky. I'll go first. When I signal, you follow."

"Signal?"

"I'll flash the Maglite," he said. "Then, while you're climbing, I'll provide cover for you. Until then, stay out of sight."

She looked over her shoulder. If the stalker meant to attack, the best time would be when they were separated. "Do you think he's still here?"

"I never took the class on how to handle a stalker, but I'd guess he gets his kicks from peeping around corners and spying on people. Be careful."

She ducked behind a rock and watched as he hiked to the edge of the Hag, found the narrow ridge and inched his way around to the wider ledge on the front. In the view from her bedroom window, that outcropping represented the Hag's gnarled hand gripping a cane. Though Ty wasn't dressed for rock climbing in his cowboy hat, clumsy belt and boots, he covered the expanse of rock with ease. On the ledge, he lay flat on his belly and flashed his light.

The wind gusted and rattled the tree branches. *Her turn.* Shadows shifted and changed shapes. As she scampered toward the Hag Stone, the skin on her back prickled, anticipating a bullet or some other object. Every glimmer of light through the trees looked like a demon racing toward her.

"You can do it," Ty called to her. "Do you need some light?"

"I can see."

In case the stalker was watching, she didn't

want to be spotlighted. At the Hag, she clung to the rough granite, broke a fingernail, scraped her knuckles. She didn't really need to hold on; the ridge was wide enough if she walked carefully. Ty had made the climb in cowboy boots, for goodness' sake. But she was disoriented on the path with the wind rattling the branches and the shadows chasing her. If she fell from here, how far would she fall? She looked down. Big mistake! Her head was spinning, and her legs were weak. Losing her balance, she faced the rock and held on tight.

He caught her hand and pulled her the rest of the way to the ledge, where she crawled onto the surface of the rock and curled up beside him. Eyes closed, she gasped for breath.

"Vertigo?" he asked.

"I've never had it before. And I'm not afraid of heights." She peeled open one eyelid and then the other. She gazed at his face, hoping she could erase the memory of the stalker with a ski mask and replace it with a mental photo of the handsome sheriff—*her* handsome sheriff. "Maybe I was a little bit scared."

"Nothing wrong with that."

"I don't like feeling helpless. So many

things in life are out of my control. What if the stalker has a gun? What if he opens fire?"

Ty placed his hand on her shoulder. "Life is uncertain, and that's scary as hell. All we can do is muddle through."

He'd taken off his hat, and the moonlight glinted in his short hair. She imagined it would be bristly and was tempted to run her hand across his head. "Do you ever get scared?"

"All the time." He adjusted his belt so he could lie sideways and prop himself up on an elbow. "I found something you might find interesting. A glove."

He had already encased the glove in a plastic evidence bag. She took it from him so she could study it carefully. Black leather with white trim and inner lining; it looked expensive. "I don't recognize it."

"If it belongs to someone who is staying at the Castle, it shouldn't be difficult to figure out who."

The wind washed over her, and a chill trembled her bones. Somehow, all roads led back to the Castle and the dinner guests. It was hard for her to imagine that one of them had been lurking around in Denver and had broken into her apartment. "How could my stalker be someone who is staying at the Castle?"

"Who else would it be?" He sat up on the rock and slapped his cowboy hat onto his head. "Who else would know which was your bedroom? Or that you could see the Hag Stone? Having a murderer and a stalker operating on the same small patch of real estate is mighty coincidental."

"But he didn't attack me. He killed Bethany."

"Your cousin. That's a connection. And a threat. Damn it, Vanessa, how many enemies do you have?"

"None!" She'd given thought to this question and was emphatic in her denial. "I'm a former English teacher and a ghostwriter. I lead a quiet life."

He stood and paced, shining the beam from his Maglite on the flat surface of the ledge and up the rock wall that led to a higher ledge. "The way I understand it, stalkers are usually motivated by sex or money or maybe revenge. Do you have any angry ex-boyfriends?"

She forced herself to sit up and rubbed at her forehead trying to think. "For the past few years of Dad's illness, I barely had time for any friends at all, much less a relationship."

"Could there be a guy who doesn't understand that you weren't interested in him? Or maybe he feels rejected. It doesn't take much to give some guys encouragement. A wink or a hug or a kiss on the cheek."

"Men are strange." She got to her feet.

He took her hand and led her across the rock to the vertical wall that was ten or twelve feet high. "Sit here. The rocks jut around this space, protecting it from view. We can't be seen unless the watcher is directly across from us, perched on the roof of the Castle."

She glanced over his shoulder to the top of the tower in the old section of the Castle. In an attempt to mimic the jagged parapets atop the ramparts of a real castle, a decorative row of stones marched along the upper wall. The stonework wasn't what caught her attention.

A light shone from the highest window in the tower—Dorothy's sewing room. The door to that room hadn't been unlocked for twelve years. "Oh, my God."

Ty followed her gaze. "I see it."

He went into immediate action. Rather than climbing down from the Hag, sprinting to the house and dashing up the staircase to the tower—a sequence of events that would take a significant chunk of time—he called his deputies on his cell phone. His instructions were swift and precise as he sent them to the tower. If they needed help accessing the room, they should talk to Mona, the housekeeper.

"Nicely done," she said.

"I was going to say that this isn't my first rodeo, but this actually is the first time I've been in pursuit of a stalker in a castle."

"How long do you think it'll take for Randall to get into the room?"

"A matter of minutes. He's already in the old section of the Castle."

Together, they stepped back, leaned against the rock wall and sat with their backs pressed against it. *A matter of minutes.* She hoped that was true. Knowing the identity of the stalker might solve everything.

The light in Aunt Dorothy's window went dark. The minutes had passed too quickly. The stalker was gone. He'd escaped.

She groaned. "Oh, no."

"We missed our chance," Ty said.

While he contacted his deputies by phone and tried to organize a long-distance search of the Castle, she turned her thoughts back to the conversation they'd had about her stalker's motives. In her perception, it seemed obvious that the stalker wasn't obsessed with her as a girlfriend. What was the second motivation Ty had mentioned? Money, the root of all evil, was a motive for just about everything... except an attack on her. She was flat broke.

Not sex. Not money. What about revenge or a grudge against her family? Maybe she was being stalked as part of a more complicated scheme—something to do with Aunt Dorothy's death. Had the stalker gone to her sewing room? Was he looking for something?

She remembered the locket with the heart and arrow design that Bethany had clutched in her hand. Aunt Dorothy was connected to many parts of this puzzle. When Vanessa initially contacted Ty, she hoped to go through the old records from the investigation into Dorothy's disappearance.

Ty finished his phone calls and stood. He stepped out onto the ledge, stared at the Castle and into the surrounding forest. His posture showed his change in attitude from hunted to hunter. Ty was going to get this guy. He reached toward her. "Give me your hand."

When he pulled her to her feet, she realized that she'd had more physical contact with Ty in the past few hours than she'd had with any other man in months. She wasn't avoiding men, far from it. But dating hadn't been possible when she was a full-time caretaker. "I wish Dad were still alive."

"Where did that thought come from?"

"Dad is never far from my memories," He died only four months ago. Sometimes, it felt like he had just left the room for a moment and would come right back. "He would have been a help in figuring out the connection to Dorothy, and he would have loved the challenge."

"Wish I could have met him."

"It's strange. I spent so much time and effort being angry with him and wishing he could have been more practical. What I miss the most are his spontaneous decisions. If I could live my life all over, I'd be more like my father."

"It's not hard to be impulsive," he said. "You pick a direction and you jump."

"Like this?" She held Ty's face in her hands. The stubble on his chin tickled her palms. Before she could consider the implications, she planted a firm kiss directly on his mouth. His lips were firm, and he tasted like…cinnamon. In shock, her brain froze while her heart raced.

She gazed up at him. *What happens after you jump?*

Chapter Eight

The next morning, Ty wakened outside beside the swimming pool on the second floor in the newer part of the Castle. Last night after searching with his deputies, he'd gone out the sliding glass doors to the flagstone terrace surrounding the pool. He'd taken off his boots and rolled up his jeans so he could dangle his feet in the water, then he'd stretched out on a lounge chair. Now, it was morning.

He lifted his hat off his face, and the sun blessed his cheeks. The Rocky Mountain vista was so beautiful that it made him wince. The pink skies of dawn outlined far-away snow-covered peaks that melted into thick pine forests with patches of aspen turning gold. Looking beyond his bare toes, Ty gazed into the rippling blue water of the pool.

He got to his feet, stretched and yawned. Behind his back, he heard the glass doors slide open. There was Vanessa wearing a long yellow bathrobe and holding a mug of coffee that was so aromatic he could smell it from twelve feet away.

"Perfect," he said. Waking up didn't get much better than this. He hoped for another kiss but doubted that would happen.

She handed him the mug and stepped back. "What are you doing out here?"

"Protecting you and your family and friends."

"From the morning sun? Do you think we're all vampires?"

"That might explain a few things." He sipped the coffee, which was just the way he liked it. No sugar. No milk. Very strong. "We spent the night patrolling and searching the Castle—Randall, Chuck and me."

"I know. I ran into Chuck in the downstairs breakfast room. He's already devoured a giant plate of waffles and Kobe beef sausage."

"Whoa! Kobe beef?"

"One of the best things about working for a celebrity chef is that we get really good quality food."

"I'm in." After setting his mug on a glass-topped table, he sat on the lounge chair to put on his socks and boots. "Our searching last night didn't turn up much. The only important thing was confirmation that you're being stalked."

"How so?"

"There was a remote-activated recorder making spooky noises and whispering your name."

"Creepy," she muttered. "That sounds like I'm being stalked by Scooby-Dum."

"Yeah, I'm pretty sure this guy isn't a pro. But that doesn't mean he's not dangerous." He stuck his foot into the boot. "The rest of the house was quiet. Everybody was snuggled in their beds with the doors locked. Mona opened Dorothy's sewing room so we could peek inside. It felt sad, like a life interrupted. Several half-finished projects, including a quilt with incredible pinks and greens, were lying around or stacked in wicker baskets. There were file cabinets and a desk."

"That room hasn't been opened in twelve years. There had to be a thick coating of dust."

"Not at all," he said. "Mona said she goes in there twice a month to wipe down the surfaces, sweep and polish the windows. Those are Simon's orders. It's almost like he's expecting Dorothy to return and rev up her sewing machine."

"He made her a shrine." Vanessa shuddered. "A bit macabre but also sweet. Did you and the deputies search in there?"

"Not a chance." He took another taste of the excellent coffee.

"Why not?"

"Same reason I didn't search in Simon's master suite. We're waiting for Special Agent Morris of the CBI and his crew of forensic experts." He was beginning to wonder if he'd made a mistake by handing over jurisdiction without a fight. Though he didn't have the necessary training or instruction, Ty had formed a connection to the victim. He wanted to know more about these suspects, to protect the innocent—like Vanessa—and arrest the guilty. "They were supposed to leave Denver at 4:00 a.m., and it's a three-to four-hour drive. They ought to be here soon."

"Which means you should go downstairs and have some breakfast." When she reached over and patted his cheek, he met her dark-eyed gaze, hoping for that second kiss. Her lips parted. She exhaled a little sigh and shook her head. "You could do with a shave, Sheriff."

By the time he got himself cleaned up and settled in the breakfast room where there were three tables and an open buffet of perfectly ripened fruit, pastries, quiches, lox and Kobe beef sausage. Coffee flowed, tea was available and there was an assortment of juices. There were cooking stations for waffles and for omelets. He stared in amazement.

Mona popped up at his elbow. "Anything I can get for you, Sheriff?"

"I think I died and went to breakfast heaven."

"I hear that a lot." She guided him to a table and pointed to a chair. "I'll bring coffee. And a waffle?"

"Okay."

Seated across from him was the agent from Aspen who Vanessa called Jack Jenkins. He was a solidly built man, a guy who probably appreciated good food. He looked up from his omelet and grinned. "I'm thinking that Simon Markham could use a full-time on-site security expert. He wouldn't even have to pay me. I'd take my wages in food."

"Tempting," Ty agreed. "What's your deal with CBI? Do you work full time for them?"

"I'm a part-time field operative. Mostly I handle the grunt work like I did last night, calling the ambulance to move the body and taking samples for DNA."

"You took fingerprints," Ty reminded him. "Did you uncover anything useful? Like criminal records or outstanding warrants?"

"Among the house staff and cooks, the backgrounds are typical for this area with minor arrests for minor offenses, a couple of drug-related things. No master criminals."

Which was to be expected. Ty was familiar with many of the locals. They were a decent bunch of people. He was more concerned with the hoity-toity visitors. "Anything I should know about the dinner guests?"

"Macy Kirov has a bunch of traffic tickets for speeding. There's a lawyer in the group—the victim's husband—so there are litigations and associated court filings. Nothing out of the ordinary."

Ty thought of the allegation that Bethany had been having an affair. "Any sign of deviant behavior, like a restraining order or a Peeping Tom complaint?"

Jenkins shrugged. "Nothing lewd or lascivious enough to register with the law. Several divorces. The only ones with kids are the Ingrams who have a grandson living with them."

Ty dropped his questioning when Mona returned to the table with a plate of two perfectly browned waffles, each topped with a big glob of melting butter. She placed a tiny pitcher of syrup beside the plate and said something. He couldn't hear her words. His entire consciousness was consumed with the sight and smell of breakfast. As he poured the golden syrup, his mouth filled with saliva.

His first bite was nearly as good as an orgasm. His eyes rolled back in his head, and he moaned in sensory delight. When he opened his eyes, he saw Vanessa walking toward them. Her honey-colored curls were pulled back in a high no-nonsense ponytail. She'd rolled up the sleeves on her white Oxford cloth shirt as though she were ready to work. Her jeans hugged her bottom. Nice.

He licked his lips. "You've got to try the waffles."

"Already have." She took a seat and gazed at him over the rim of her coffee mug. "Agent Morris and his crew are approaching the front entrance."

Ty shot a glance toward Jenkins. "I'm going to pretend that I didn't hear what she just said. This waffle needs to be savored."

"I'm with you," Jenkins murmured.

"Fine," Vanessa said. "I'll get them settled in the corner conference room off the Grand Hall."

She flounced off, and he refocused his attention on the waffle with maple syrup and creamy butter. After he polished off the first waffle, he set his fork down on the plate and looked over at Jenkins. "I guess we'd better go and meet your boss."

"I'm in no hurry. I don't have anything definitive to tell him. All the data I gathered from last night is in a written report."

"Can I get a copy?"

"Already done." He dipped into a wallet attached to his utility belt and extracted a computer flash drive, which he placed beside Ty's breakfast plate. "It's a duplicate of what I'll be handing over to Morris. I knew you'd want to be kept informed."

This cheerful cooperation surprised Ty. Jenkins's boss had been demanding and hostile, but the Aspen operative was downright friendly. Vanessa might have thought he was a jerk, but Ty liked the guy. "Thanks."

"I've heard good stuff about you. People trust you. They think you're honest, smart and not afraid to work hard." Jenkins settled his cowboy hat on his head, hitched up his belt and headed in the direction Vanessa had gone. "Good luck with Morris."

After Ty finished his second waffle and downed his second mug of coffee, he thanked Mona for her hospitality and went toward the conference room where Agent Morris had established his headquarters. A whole lot of electronics and computer equipment were spread across two long tables. A female agent with her hair cut almost as short as his worked on a laptop with an attached extra-large screen that showed an array of driver's license photos for the dinner guests. Apparently, Morris was thinking along the same line as Ty, suspecting that the killer was one of the people who had stayed at the Castle last night.

Vanessa waved him over to where she was sitting with Morris. When she introduced the two men, Ty recognized the macho challenge in the agent's aggressive handshake and confrontational squint through narrow eyes. His smile was a sneer. His greeting was a growl deep in his throat. Ty was taller, younger and probably stronger than Morris, but he wasn't looking for a fight.

Though he hadn't been in the armed services and had only been a deputy for a couple of months before the sheriff died, Ty understood the need for an appointed leader who took charge and gave orders. Chain of command was a smart way of handling a complicated investigation with a lot of moving parts. It was a tough job—one he didn't want.

"How can I help, Agent Morris?"

"Vanessa filled me in on the basics of her interviews and gave me her record of the data she collected. They all claim to have alibis. No surprise there. I'm inclined to agree with the basic assumption that Bethany's murder was a result of her own foolish infidelity."

Ty hated the way Morris had framed his theory. As if Bethany taking a lover made her fair game for a murderer? Ty said, "Whether or not she had an affair, the murder wasn't her fault. She didn't cause her own death."

Morris gave a derisive snort. "Vanessa, did I say that?"

"Not in so many words." She was better at politics than Ty. "Do you have any information about who she was having an affair with?"

"That's what forensics will show us. My team is already in the master suite, going over the murder scene. We'll find something. We always do." He was confident…maybe over-confident. "In the meantime, I need to interrogate the witnesses. I'll use that nifty recording area you have already set up in the library."

"Sorry." Her tone chilled by several degrees. "I need that room for my work with Simon."

"Ghostwriting for a celebrity chef? Do you really think that's more important than a murder investigation?"

"I don't, but Simon does." Her voice was sheer ice. She whipped out her cell phone. "Why don't I just call him and see what he thinks? Like most important men who regularly appear on TV, he's not known for his patience, but I'm sure he won't mind the inconvenience."

"Never mind," Morris muttered.

Ty sensed that he and Vanessa were about to be booted out of the investigation. No matter how obnoxious Morris was, Ty wanted access to the information uncovered by the CBI and that meant making nice with these agents. Ty dug into a pouch on his utility belt and pulled out the plastic evidence bag with the single glove inside and dropped it on the table. "There's another track to this investigation that needs to be investigated. Last night, Vanessa and I found this glove on the Hag Stone at the rear of the house where it had been dropped by her stalker."

Morris picked up the evidence bag and stared through the clear plastic. "Okay, Vanessa, why do you think you're being stalked?"

She ran through the story of her stalker, paying particular attention to the fact that she'd filed a police report after he broke into her Denver apartment. "Last night was the first time I've seen him since I moved to the Castle. I left my bedroom and found Ty. Together, we ran to the place where the stalker had been standing. He was gone."

Morris shrugged. "Why do you think this stalker is connected to your cousin's murder?"

"When Ty and I looked around, we saw a light from a bedroom in the tower. It came from Aunt Dorothy's sewing room. As far as I knew, the door to that room hadn't been opened in twelve years."

Morris swiveled to face Ty. "Did you catch the guy?"

"I called my deputies who were inside the Castle. They went to the sewing room, but they were too late. They found Mona, the housekeeper, and she unlocked the room."

"It wasn't dusty at all," Vanessa said with a sense of wonder. "Mona has been keeping it clean all these years on Simon's order."

"I had my deputies seal off the room with crime scene tape," Ty said. "Nobody went inside. I wanted to leave it for your forensic team."

"What do you think we'll find?" Morris asked.

"I'm hoping for evidence that would lead to the stalker, but I have my doubts." Ty folded his arms across his chest. "The appearance of the stalker seemed staged. First, he appears and calls attention to himself to lure Vanessa outside. We found a remote-controlled microphone in her bedroom, Then he drops a glove where we'll be sure to find it. And he flashes a light in Aunt Dorothy's sewing room At least, I think it was the same guy."

"A setup," Morris said. "Good thinking."

"I'm just saying…we need to be skeptical about evidence from the stalker. But we also need to investigate. He's a real guy, a real threat. If he was the one in Aunt Dorothy's sewing room, he's not the only one pointing to her."

"Who else?" Morris demanded.

Ty unfolded his arms and stuck one hand

into his pocket. "Bethany told her husband that she had reason to believe she was entitled to an inheritance from Aunt Dorothy's estate."

"And what did Lowell Burke say?"

"He didn't think his wife's idea had merit."

"Burke is a lawyer. I've never known one of those bloodsuckers to turn their back on a potential cash payout." He dropped a condescending pat on Ty's shoulder. "Your suspicions are duly noted, and I will send my forensic team up to the sewing room, but I think you were right when you called this a setup. Somebody is playing games with you."

Ty didn't call murder a game. "I want to be informed of your forensic results."

"Sure thing, son. And don't you worry, we'll solve this crime. And I'll bet the killer is Bethany's boyfriend."

Son? Ty was maybe ten years younger than this agent, and he didn't like being treated like a kid. He straightened his shoulders, sucked in his gut and prepared to be a good soldier who obeyed orders.

At the same time, he closed his fingers around the gold necklace in his pocket, which he now had tucked away in an evidence bag. This locket had been clutched in Bethany's hand when she was killed. It was important. Central to the crime. And Ty would be damned if he shared this piece of jewelry with Morris. Maybe Ty wasn't so readily obedient after all. Maybe he was cut out to be the boss. He needed to try harder.

In a residence as large as the Castle, Ty didn't think it would be hard to find privacy, but it took smart logistics to arrange a meeting with Vanessa in a place where they wouldn't be overheard. At the swimming pool before lunch, he stood at the far edge of the pool, waiting for her and watching through the sliding glass doors as several of the guests made their way toward the staircase that led down to the area where lunch would be served. From the cooking aromas, he guessed the food would be some kind of pasta with garlic bread.

The Ingrams walked together, hand in hand. After all their years together, there was no need to talk. They seemed like a sweet couple, but Ty knew they had their share of problems with their druggy grandson and George's binge drinking, as well as Martha's accusation that he was having an affair.

Gloria Gable stalked down the hall behind

them, somehow managing to turn jeans and a plaid flannel shirt into a fashion statement.

Then came the Kirov couple. Yuri had been identified as the owner of the glove Ty had found on the Hag Stone, which didn't make sense. Yuri might have been Bethany's lover, but he didn't have any connection to Vanessa. There was no discernible reason for him to stalk her in Denver. More than ever, the glove and the arrival of the stalker appeared to be a setup, a distraction from the real crime. Speaking of distraction… Macy dragged all the attention to herself with her booming voice and flashy clothes. Today, she was dressed in swirls of tie-dye with enough colorful beads to impersonate a Mardi Gras float.

When Vanessa slipped through the sliding glass doors, he felt profound relief. She was still wearing her white shirt with the rolled-up sleeves and her jeans. He noticed her oversize silver belt buckle that appeared to be some kind of award for barrel racing.

He commented on the buckle. "I thought you were only a kid when you left the mountains, but it looks like you were old enough for rodeo."

"Little Britches Rodeo," she said. "I was

nine, and the junior barrel race wasn't even a sanctioned event. I've seen what the adult racers can do, and they're amazing. I wouldn't dream of putting myself in the same class with them."

"Did you win?"

"Damn right, I did." She flashed a cocky grin. "Why did you want to see me?"

"I'm getting bounced out of here. Morris made it clear that he doesn't need my help. He told me to send the deputies home, and I should leave, too. But he wants us back after dark to keep an eye on the Castle and make sure nobody else gets hurt."

"That's not right." Her voice was firm. "He can't come in here and start ordering people around. Who does he think he is?"

"An agent for the Colorado Bureau of Investigation. And I gave him jurisdiction." Ty had been impressed with the work done by the CBI, including deep research on the witnesses. The woman on the computer turned up clue after clue. "After last night, I'm concerned about your safety. If anything weird turns up, give me a call. Later tonight, we should sneak into Aunt Dorothy's sewing room for a look around. I'll check back with you after dinner."

"Is that a date?"

"Not unless your idea of a good time is breaking crime scene tape and poking around in a room that's been unoccupied for twelve years."

"Actually," she said, "that sounds better than a lot of dates I've had."

Chapter Nine

Vanessa's next recording session with Simon was scheduled for two o'clock, which left her with some free time. She would have liked to follow Ty around the house but didn't want to look like an adoring puppy dog. She'd been out of the dating game long enough to be unsure of what came next. A setting of boundaries or a breaking down of walls, she didn't know which.

She decided to join the others for lunch. This might be an awkward meal, but the food was always great when Simon was in the kitchen. The houseguests—who had been ordered not to leave until after they spoke with Morris—gathered at tables in the casual breakfast room.

Vanessa had found herself seated with Ice Queen Chloe, the Ingrams and Macy Kirov. Yuri Kirov had taken a place at another table with Burke, Jack Jenkins from Aspen and Keith Gable. The men were talking low, and it sounded like the topic was real estate and business.

Hoping to break the ice, Vanessa turned to Macy. "I like your colorful beads. The purple and green make me think of New Orleans."

"Not too garish?"

"Not a bit."

"I've been thinking about starting my own fashion line for big women like me." She craned her neck. "I should talk to Gloria. An international model ought to have good feedback on fashion trends. Is she here?"

"Oh, Gloria doesn't eat lunch," Chloe informed them as she picked at her small salad. "She brought her own special formula for a smoothie cleanse. Simon has been trying to duplicate the health benefits and make it taste better."

"How's that going?" Vanessa asked.

Chloe made a face. "Not tasty."

"I've got to have protein with every meal. Nothing beats a ribeye." Macy nudged Doc Ingram's shoulder. "Am I right, George?"

He nodded. The conversation sputtered along for another ten minutes while they served themselves from family-sized containers of salad, fruit and penne in cream sauce with prosciutto and Parmigiano-Reggiano. Great food. Lousy chatter.

Macy blurted, "Okay, folks, we need to talk about the elephant in the room. Somebody— maybe somebody right here at these tables— is a cold-blooded murderer."

"Not necessarily," Jenkins, the only actual cop among them, said. "I've been going through the data from surveillance cameras, and it looks to me like we're missing a lot. It's very possible that the killer sneaked into the house from outside."

"I don't think so," Chloe said. "We have every exit covered."

"But not every window or other access point, like the cellar or the swimming pool or the balconies. Your security is good, ma'am, but not airtight. In a house as big as this one, a skilled intruder can always find a way to break in."

Macy shook her head. "Should that make me feel better or worse? I hate thinking that one of us killed poor Bethany. But I don't like imagining an intruder creeping through the halls, waiting to attack."

Chloe picked up her water glass and tapped her spoon against the side. "We shouldn't discuss the crime. Agent Morris asked that we not chat among ourselves."

"She's right," Jenkins said. "Leave the crime-solving to the professionals."

Vanessa heard the echo of condescending advice from Morris. *Leave it to us. You don't know what you're doing.* She couldn't pretend to be an expert on fingerprints and DNA, but she could guess at motives, and she knew more about this house and this family than anyone else. She was born a Whitman.

And she intended to find out everything she could, starting with anything about Aunt Dorothy. Her disappearance and death were a puzzle that needed to be unlocked.

IN THE LIBRARY, Vanessa prepared her recording corner for Simon. He liked to have fresh water, which she brought up in the dumbwaiter from the baking kitchen below. And he liked a choice of seats, ranging from a straight-back wooden chair at the table to a leather recliner that matched the sofa. Gathering enough information for a memoir could be hard work, especially since Simon didn't have a good idea of the image he wanted to portray. She'd suggested a few other memoirs from celebrity chefs that he could read, but he wasn't interested. Like most people, he preferred skimming the text, studying the recipes and savoring the delicious photos of food that decorated the pages.

Today, he entered the library and went directly to the dumbwaiter that he activated with the flick of a switch. He seemed nervous. Who wouldn't be with a murder in his bedroom and the CBI all over his house? His face was more flushed than usual.

"I have a treat," he said, "that might make it easier to understand my early life. Are you ready? It's Neapolitan pizza."

She recognized the pizza made with tomato, mozzarella and basil, and she enjoyed the rich, spicy aroma. Truly, this was one of her faves. "But I just had lunch."

"This isn't for eating. The pizza has a story. It originated in Naples and is red, white and green, like the Italian flag."

She decided to play along. "What does this wonderful pizza have to do with your life story?"

"So many of the great chefs talk about how they learned how to cook with their grandma or mama. They have warm, folksy stories that people can relate to. And so, *voila!* When I was a kid, I spent several summers with my sweet Jewish grandmother, my *zaidy*, who lived in Naples, Italy. Here's a photo."

Dressed in 1980s chic—a mini-skirt and sequined jacket with padded shoulders—his *zaidy* was the furthest thing from a kindly old lady who toiled in the kitchen to make pizza for her grandson. "She's beautiful," Vanessa said.

"But not heartwarming."

"That depends." The photo had triggered a spark in her imagination that might become a full-fledged concept. "Here's the thing, Simon. You've got to be true to yourself. Let those other chefs have their supposedly humble beginnings. Your grandma was cosmopolitan and classy."

He nodded, reluctantly proud of her. "She was."

"And when she took you out to eat, I'll bet you went to great places."

"Absolutely. And she usually knew the chef."

"Think about it, Simon. Maybe she didn't put the mixing bowl in your hand and teach you the secrets of nutmeg and cilantro, but she showed you what great cooking was really about."

Vanessa could almost see a light bulb over his head. *He got it.*

"Cosmopolitan," he murmured. "She made sure I wore a suit and bow tie. I had to sit up straight. And I had to compliment the chef. *Magnifico!*"

He rattled off several charming stories about places he'd gone and food he'd eaten with his stylish grandma in Naples while Vanessa sat back and let the recorder do the work. She used a wheel cutter to slice off a piece of the Neapolitan pizza, which was fresh, tasty and great. She nibbled, munching, sipping water and listening. When Simon wasn't forcing himself to be somebody else, he was interesting and had a cool background.

As he continued to talk, he picked up steam and turned a deeper shade of crimson. He rose from the chair at the table and paced. "This is good stuff."

"You bet," she said.

"Where do we go from here?"

"I think we have enough for today. I'll transcribe these recordings, then you can look them over and decide which are the best to include."

"I could take a trip to Naples and revisit some of these restaurants. Dorothy and I traveled there. She met my *zaidy*, and they hit it off."

Now was the moment when Vanessa could make the transition to her own agenda. She reached forward and deliberately turned off the recorder. "There's something we need to discuss off the record…about Dorothy and how she died."

His back was toward her, and she saw him cringe. His shoulders tensed. "I don't have anything more to say. You've already heard what happened."

"Let me see if I have it right." When Vanessa was growing up, this was the basic story her father told. "Aunt Dorothy went for a ride one afternoon in November when the weather was nice. She didn't come home but her horse returned to the barn after dark. Teams from S&R went out to look for her. She couldn't be found. A few days later, winter hit. A blizzard. The ground was covered with a blanket of snow."

"We didn't find her remains until after the spring thaw," Simon said. "End of story."

"That doesn't feel like a conclusion. I still have questions. Was there DNA testing to be sure the remains belonged to Dorothy?"

"Yes."

"Among the remains, what was found?"

"I never saw them." Stiffly, he sat at the table. His posture was as tense as his words. "You'd have to talk to Doc Ingram or Keith. There was a skull, some ribs, a femur and other bones."

"Was there a cause of death?"

"Trauma to the head."

Just like Bethany. What was the connection? Why couldn't Vanessa see what was missing? "This is painful for you to talk about, and I'm sorry. But I need to find the truth. The sheriff can give me access to the county records that pertain to her death, and I can talk to Doc Ingram. He was the coroner at the time."

"Stop playing games with me, Vanessa. You already know what you're going to find."

Simon was usually aggressive and sometimes scary, but she felt sorry for him. "I don't know what you're talking about."

"Dorothy and I had been going through a rough patch in our marriage. Simplicity was a success in terms of reviews from critics and customers, but I was losing money every month. There wasn't a large enough client base in this area. Keith and I had begun talks about the Simple Simon's franchise. Dorothy hated the idea. She said that if I started another venture, we'd have less time together."

"Which was probably true," Vanessa said.

"She said she had enough family money for us to live comfortably for the rest of our lives."

Also true. Aunt Dorothy wasn't a fool. "Did you have a problem with that?"

He slanted a glance toward her. "I might be old-fashioned, but I've always believed that the man should be the breadwinner. On the day Dorothy went for her ride, we argued. I went to Simplicity for the rest of the day. I should have been home waiting for her, should have responded sooner when she didn't come back. I could have stopped her."

He collapsed facedown across the table. His shoulders trembled as he silently wept.

She came around beside him and rested her hand on his back. "You can't blame yourself."

"My Dorothy," he whispered in a barely audible voice. "My darling, my love. My Dorothy committed suicide."

Chapter Ten

Vanessa had been standing at her bedroom window looking out at the sheen of moonlight on the face of the Hag Stone while she recited this part of the story for Ty. Though Simon had told her about the great tragedy of his life hours ago, his words still echoed in her head. "Suicide," she said. "My aunt Dorothy killed herself."

She whirled and faced Ty who sat in her desk chair with his long legs stretched out in front of him. They'd both been biding their time until he returned to the Castle for his late-night guard duty. As soon as he'd checked in with his deputies, he came to her room. She'd expected him to look tired, but he didn't show the signs of exhaustion. He must have used his time away from the Castle to go home and nap, which was smart. She should have done the same instead of relying on nervous energy to keep herself alert.

"Are you okay?" he asked.

"I guess so. But suicide?"

"Are you sure?"

"Doc Ingram did the autopsy. He verified suicide by gunshot wound to the head. It's hard to believe."

"Did you know Dorothy well?"

"Not really."

From her dim memories and her father's recollections, Vanessa had the impression that Dorothy had been a strong, willful woman who knew what she wanted and wasn't afraid to go after it. In photographs, she looked confident with her chin lifted and her gaze directly facing the camera.

"I'm guessing there's more to this story," he said. "What else did Simon tell you?"

"He didn't want to see the remains."

"I understand," Ty said. "Her body was exposed to the elements for months, and the scavengers would have picked the bones. When I was working for Search and Rescue, we advised the survivors to think long and hard before making the decision to view the body. Sometimes, it's less painful to remember your loved one in better circumstances."

She agreed. One of the reasons she was glad her father decided on cremation was because she couldn't bear to see him lying helpless in a coffin, ravaged by the cancer that had reduced his once vigorous physique to skin and bones. It wasn't fair that her last image of him would be so sad. "Simon didn't have her cremated. Her bones were sealed in a small wooden box."

"Was there a suicide note?" Ty asked.

"I asked about that, and Simon said no."

"There are lots of reasons why it wouldn't be found. If she'd taken a note outside, it could have been destroyed in the weather. Or if she left it somewhere in the house, it could have been misplaced."

"Anyway," she said with a sigh, "Keith Gable was the person who stepped up and took care of things after they found the remains. He and Doc Ingram came to the Castle and told Simon that DNA testing had been done, and Dorothy's death was labeled suicide. She shot herself in the head." She remembered how miserable Simon had looked when he told her. Even now, twelve years later, his eyes were red-rimmed, and his lower lip trembled. "He was heartbroken."

"I'm surprised you didn't know about the suicide. After all, you're Dorothy's niece."

"Simon wanted to keep it quiet. He felt guilty on several levels, blamed himself for her unhappiness and thought he should have been more attentive. I was in college and hadn't seen her or Simon in years. I didn't attend the memorial service, which was held after Christmas before the body was discovered."

She should have gone to the memorial as a representative of the Whitman family. Dad had been out of the country; he didn't make it, either. A few years ago, when he knew his cancer was terminal, they talked about his early years with Dorothy. He respected his older sister and resented her at the same time because she was the eldest and, therefore, claimed control over the family's wealth after their parents died.

"Her suicide would have been reported on official documents," Ty said. "George Ingram as coroner had to state the cause of death. It wasn't a secret."

"You're right." She crossed the room and hopped up on the desk beside him. "As soon as I did some poking around, I would have found the facts. It doesn't seem like Dorothy's suicide is connected to Bethany's murder or to the stalker."

"But why would the stalker creep into her sewing room." He stuck his hand into his pocket and pulled out the locket in the evidence bag. "And why was Bethany holding this when she died?"

"We need more research," she said. "We have to keep looking."

"Here's a thought." He tilted his head to look up at her. "Suicide usually negates the payout on insurance policies. Could someone have faked the suicide to cheat Simon out of his inheritance?"

"That's the first time I've heard of somebody faking a suicide."

"It's a stretch," he said.

"And it doesn't apply. When they found the remains, Simon and Keith were already on the verge of starting the Simple Simon's franchise restaurants. He used the Castle and other properties as collateral for loans."

"Still, it might be worthwhile to check into those old insurance policies and Aunt Dorothy's will. Simon might be heartbroken, but money is still a motive." As he rose to his feet, he dropped his arm around her shoulder and pulled her off the desk. "Let's go search that mysterious sewing room."

She snuggled against his chest. They fit together nicely with her head nestled in the crook of his neck. "And what will we be looking for?"

"We'll know when we see it."

When he gave her a squeeze, she lingered, hoping for more. Like it or not, there was a relationship developing between them.

Ty PAUSED OUTSIDE the locked door to Aunt Dorothy's room. Yellow crime scene tape crisscrossed on the door frame. He dug into one of the pouches on his utility belt and took out two pairs of blue latex gloves and two sets of disposable booties. "We've got to wear these. The CBI forensic team has already processed the room, and I don't want to contaminate."

"Did they find anything?"

"The only fingerprints were from Mona. There were smudges, probably left behind by the stalker who was wearing gloves. Other than that, spotless."

"And how do we get inside?"

He tried the handle and the door opened easily. "I guess the CBI doesn't consider this to be important evidence. Try not to tear down the tape."

She ducked between the yellow strips, and he followed. Inside the sewing room, he closed the door and turned on the overhead light. The room was large but not massive with a smooth-topped square table in the center and the actual sewing machine at a long table under a pegboard array of different colored thread in a spectrum from red to violet. The atmosphere was feminine, efficient and somewhat weird with two mannequin dummy torsos standing together near the window as though they were peeking out at the forested hillsides.

If he hadn't known Vanessa and Dorothy were related, he could have guessed at the connection from the organized arrangement of the sewing room. "Do you remember this place from when you were a kid?"

"I loved playing in here while Aunt Dorothy sewed."

Vanessa stood before a wall of bins. Each space was filled with see-through plastic containers. Some held equipment, like scissors, bobbins and tape measures. Other boxes—in several different sizes—were for zippers or patterns or smaller containers filled with buttons. Most were for fabric in different colors and textures.

The layout was impressive, and it was obvious that Vanessa approved. She tapped with her fingers in blue latex gloves on one box after another and mumbled descriptions that he didn't understand, like *chartreuse charmeuse* and *Pepto-pink chiffon*. He heard her humming as she approached the huge closet along another wall. Inside the hanging space were several garment bags—all clear plastic. Vanessa unzipped one and stepped back to admire the slinky sequined midnight blue dress inside.

"Dorothy would have looked gorgeous in this," she murmured. "The only thing she enjoyed about formal events was the chance to get all dressed up. I'll bet she was working on this for the Annual Ski Ball at the start of the season in Aspen."

Preparing an outfit for a fancy event didn't sound like the action of a woman who was contemplating suicide. He rapped on the table in the center of the room. "What's this used for?"

"Take a guess." She grinned. "And here's a clue. It's not for autopsies."

"I know that." He would have recognized

an autopsy table, which was usually stainless steel with gutters on each side to catch the blood. "But this table could be used for dissection."

"Aunt Dorothy would never allow messy body parts to clutter her room. She didn't even allow peanut butter snacks in here." She pulled open a drawer and took out a pair of scissors with a jagged edge. "Guess again."

"Deformed scissors?"

"Pinking shears." She returned them to their drawer and embraced the table from end to end. "This is a cutting table for laying out patterns and trimming edges. The last time I saw it, Dorothy was finishing the green-and-blue-patterned quilt in my bedroom."

For the first time, he had a sense of Vanessa being connected to the legendary Whitman family. She and Aunt Dorothy had been cut from the same cloth, and that unintentional pun made him wonder. From what he knew about Vanessa during the last few years, she'd been through hell. Had she ever thought of killing herself like Aunt Dorothy?

"Are you ever depressed?" he asked.

"Everybody gets blue. Why do you ask?"

Since he didn't have psychological training on profiling, Ty had to just come out and say what he was thinking. "I've heard that some types of behavior have a genetic cause, like alcoholism or addiction. And this room makes me think you're very similar to your aunt."

"Okay."

Her gaze was doubtful and sort of confused. He wasn't doing a good job of explaining. His tongue felt too thick for his mouth, and his words were clumsy. No point in sugarcoating, he cleared his throat. "Have you ever thought of killing yourself?"

"Of course not." Her dark eyes flared. She slammed the pinking shears drawer in front of her, pivoted and steamed away from the cutting table to pace around the room. When she stopped in front of the dummy torsos, he thought she might attack them like punching bags.

She glared at him. "You might think that because we lived in a castle, the Whitman family is too rich and entitled to deal with real life, but you'd be wrong. I come from generations of strong women and men who made their way in the west when everything was against them. We don't quit. And we don't give up."

"What really happened to Aunt Dorothy?" he asked.

"I can't imagine that she took a gun and blew her brains out." She gasped and her eyes went wide as she stared at him. "Wait! I remember something. This might be important."

Vanessa dove into the closet and shoved the garment bags aside, revealing a small built-in wall safe with a combination lock. She leaned down and spun the dial. With little hesitation, she flipped from one number to the next.

"How are you remembering this?" he asked.

"It's my birthday."

She and her aunt had a deeper bond than first suggested. He supposed that it made sense. Dorothy had been childless and in her forties, married to an ambitious man who sometimes acted like a child himself. Vanessa would have been an adorable little girl to dress in ruffles and bows. "What's in the safe?"

"I'm hoping to find documents," she said. "Maybe the insurance policy or her will. She also kept her handgun in here. A Walther PPK like James Bond."

When the final number clicked and she

reached for the handle, he stopped her. "Hold on. I want to document this." He aimed the camera on his phone. "Open it."

She tugged on the handle, and the door swung open. Inside were two boxes: one for jewelry and a gun case. Vanessa removed the jewelry box, which held a few classic pieces with glittering diamonds and rubies set in white gold. "The only time I saw her wear these was at a rodeo where the gems were totally inappropriate and very cool."

"Why would she do that?"

"She told me that one of the new residents intended to race a thoroughbred and trounce all the locals. The diamonds and rubies were her way of reminding people that new people were always welcome but the Whitman family reigned supreme from the Castle."

She had a strange upbringing. On one hand, she'd been taught that she wasn't entitled to special privilege. On the other, she should think of herself as local royalty. Then her parents left, and Vanessa was just another kid on a playground.

He nodded toward the gun case. "Open it."

"I expect it to be empty." She flipped the latch. "If Dorothy committed suicide, this would be the weapon she used."

But the Walther PPK was still in the case.

"Don't touch it," he cautioned. "There might be prints."

"This gun is more evidence that Dorothy didn't commit suicide. If she intended to kill herself, why not use her own weapon? Why leave it here?"

"In twelve years," he said, "no one found the weapon. Why not?"

"I have an answer. I was the only one who knew about the safe. That's why the combination was my birthday."

"We need to dig deeper. Before I present this information to Morris tomorrow morning, I want as much detail as possible. Put the gun and jewelry back the way you found them, and let's go through the rest of the room."

Dorothy's intense organization made it easier to search. They could easily shuffle through the contents of each bin. With no extra clutter to distract, the contents of each drawer were obvious. Vanessa added her own commentary about what the fabrics had been used to create and the best technique for zippers, but he was focused. And his diligence paid off.

He held up a five-by-eight spiral notebook.

"I've seen something like this before. On the desk in your office."

"To-do lists," Vanessa said. "I'd forgotten that Dorothy was the one who got me started on that habit. List the main jobs to accomplish day by day. The back is for ongoing projects."

He held the book out of her reach. "Do you always cross out every item on your list?"

"Mostly, but I'm not a fanatic about it. These detailed lists were more important when I was teaching school. When Dad was sick, the lists got chaotic. I'd make a detailed plan, then he'd need an immediate procedure."

"You started making lists again."

"When I took the job as Simon's ghost, and I also have a calendar with deadlines." She snatched the book from him and started thumbing through the pages. "She's got a lot of info on the Aspen Ski Ball. Apparently, Dorothy was in charge of the silent auction."

Ty read over her shoulder. These notations described the life of a woman who was socially active and had a full life. He didn't see a hint of depression or the kind of deep sadness he would associate with suicide.

Vanessa flipped to the back and pointed emphatically to the last few pages. "Do you see what this is? It's the start of a list for Christmas presents. The plan of a suicidal woman? I don't think so."

"Hold up the book so I can take a picture. We're not removing it from this room." He'd already swiped the locket. If he tampered with more evidence, Morris might shut him out of the investigation altogether.

Vanessa replaced the notebook on a stand beside the sewing machine and went to a bulletin board with several photographs pinned haphazardly. "I'm surprised to see so many photos of me."

She was a cute kid with her golden hair pulled back in braids or ponytails. A constellation of freckles dotted her cheeks. Even in a photograph, she looked like she was in motion—the kind of kid who was always dashing from place to place and back again.

"That's me in a Halloween costume, dressed like a green Martian." She pointed to the pictures, one after another. "There's me in a dress that Dorothy made. And that one is my Little Britches rodeo costume."

She unpinned one from the board and held it. "This is Dad and Dorothy. They were probably eight and eleven. They're standing by the gravestone of Mr. Fluffball, a yellow cat."

"They decorated it with yellow graffiti paint and blue flowers."

"There's a whole story about their journey to transport Fluffball to his final resting place and digging the grave and Fluffball's funeral. Dad wrote a poem about that day."

When she looked up at him, a tear slipped over her eyelid and down her cheek. "That's the place, Ty. Fluffball's grave, that's where I need to scatter Dad's ashes."

"That feels right to me."

She sighed. "Feels like I'm finally coming home."

Chapter Eleven

After spending the night on patrol in the Castle and catching an early morning nap in one of the spare bedrooms, Ty brushed his teeth, splashed water on his face and went downstairs. Though it was only a few minutes after six o'clock, one of his deputies was already at a table in the breakfast room, drinking coffee and casting longing glances toward the kitchen.

Ty filled his mug. "What do you think, McNally? Is breakfast today going to be as good as yesterday?"

"I'm hoping." He was a single guy, skinny as a stick. Women loved to feed him. "Mona said it was empanadas, frittatas and fruit salad."

The aroma of deep-fried dough, onions and peppers wafted from the open kitchen door. Ty asked, "Anything to report from last night?"

"It was quiet, except for you and Vanessa banging around in the upstairs sewing room. Did you find any, um, new evidence?"

Ignoring the innuendo, Ty answered, "I think so."

He hoped Agent Morris would think the same way. The CBI was unlikely to abandon the more direct investigation into Bethany's murder, but Ty was certain the cold case had relevance. He rose from the table. "I'll be back. Enjoy your breakfast."

He crossed the Grand Hall and went toward the conference room where the CBI had their headquarters. When he peeked inside, he saw cop clutter scattered across the tabletops—files, photos and documents. Whiteboards had been set up and scribbled on. Photos of witnesses, suspects and dinner guests were posted on a corkboard. He didn't like seeing Vanessa's picture among the others.

At the end of one table, Agent Morris stared at a computer screen. His heavy shoulders slouched as though his spine had folded like an accordion. The gray at his temples seemed to have spread, and he was wearing a pair of wire-frame glasses. Ty suspected that the investigation wasn't sailing smoothly ahead but reminded himself not to gloat.

He took a seat beside the CBI agent and said, "I see you found the coffee."

"A damn fine cup of joe."

"I recommend the breakfast."

Morris leaned back in his chair, took off his glasses and rubbed his forehead. "You came here because you want to hear what we've picked up in the way of evidence. Right?"

"Yes, sir." Ty had thought Morris was more dedicated to furthering his career than to solving the murder, but he was wrong. "As long as I'm here at the crack of dawn, I also want to compliment you for getting a head start on the day."

"Here's the headline," Morris said. "Bethany was having an affair. We've contacted friends in LA who confirm that she was messing around. They also told us that her husband has a honey on the side. No names or descriptions, but Bethany's guy is wealthy."

"Do any of the witnesses or suspects stand out?"

"I'm leaning toward Kirov and Gable."

"Did you learn anything more from the background checks?" Ty asked.

"Nothing."

"Blood spatter analysis?" At the very least, Ty hoped to learn something from the experienced forensic team.

Morris balanced his glasses on the tip of his nose, tapped a few keys on his laptop and brought up a sketch of the floorplan for the murder scene that included major pieces of furniture. "You can see from the spatter that Bethany was initially hit near the bathroom using the decorative urn with the heavy marble base. Clearly, a weapon of opportunity. The killer was likely right-handed. Could have been a man or a woman. In reconstructing the crime, we believe Bethany and the murderer argued, the killer grabbed the vase and swung."

"Bethany wasn't initially unconscious," Ty said.

"She attempted to crawl away, dragging herself toward the bed. The second blow finished her off."

"Cause of death?"

"We won't have the full autopsy for a few days. The body is being transferred to the forensic pathology lab we use in Denver. The hospital in Aspen issued a preliminary death certificate and ran a tox screen to catch any toxins that might disappear in the blood."

"Drugs?"

"No drugs. No poisons."

Ty eased into his next topic. "Did your forensic people find evidence in Aunt Dorothy's sewing room?"

"No prints. No fibers. It was impeccably clean." He took off his glasses and studied Ty. "I heard that you and Vanessa made your own visit to the sewing room."

"Who told you?"

"Simon himself. He was having trouble sleeping, especially since he couldn't stay in his own bed. He wandered through the Castle and saw you and Vanessa tiptoeing up the staircase."

"I thought there might be something in that room to jog Vanessa's memory about her aunt's death."

"And?" Morris arched his eyebrows. "Was there?"

"We uncovered information that negates the cause of death as suicide."

Morris sat up straight in his chair and scowled. "It was twelve years ago. Does it really matter if it was an accident or suicide?"

"I believe it does," Ty said. He ran through the sequence of events, showing how Dorothy had gone from accident victim to missing person to the bloody remains of a suicide.

"And here's why I can't believe that's true. Number one—Dorothy was planning ahead, putting the finishing touches on a gown to wear at the Aspen Ski Ball. Number two— her to-do list was up to date, and she was planning her Christmas presents. Number three—her Walther PPK is still in the safe. If she intended to kill herself with a gunshot to the head, why not take her own pistol?"

Morris nodded slowly. "You made good points, especially about the gun locked in the safe, and Dorothy's death probably deserves more investigation, but I still don't see how it's related to Bethany's murder."

This was where the tidy house of cards Ty had constructed fell apart. He didn't know how Dorothy was connected, but he was certain that she was. "I want to keep investigating. It would help if I could have access to some of your people, especially the computer experts, like Liz Hurtado."

"As long as you don't interfere with other evidence, I have no problem with that."

"Thank you, sir."

Morris had changed his tune. When they first met, he was all brass and bluster, warning Ty to keep out of his way. After dealing with a full day of frustration, his rhythm had softened to a slower beat.

"Matter of fact," Morris said, "you and your deputies don't need to patrol the Castle tonight. I'm sending half my team back to Denver, and the rest of us—including me—will stay here. Also, I'm giving permission to the house guests to go home. They need to be accessible and stay in state, but they don't have to be at the Castle."

In a way, that was progress, but Ty didn't like it. He worried about Vanessa. Would she be safe with a less visible police presence?

WHEN VANESSA ROLLED out of bed at ten o'clock, she found a text from Ty on her cell phone. He was doing research on court records and wanted to meet her in the horse barn behind the Castle at three in the afternoon.

The timing was perfect. She had an interview with Simon and Keith at one. After that, she was free. Going for a horseback ride seemed like a great idea. During the months she'd been living at the Castle, she'd only taken the horses out once a week or less. Yesterday, when she'd been talking about her stellar career in Little Britches, she remembered the physical rush that came when she rode hard and fast. And the subtle joy of sitting astride a horse and pacing through a forest, watching the clouds float across the skies and listening to the whir of the wind through pine boughs.

She texted back with an all-caps affirmative and a happy face. Too much? But she wanted Ty to know how much she appreciated his help. If it weren't for him, Agent Morris would have given her a pat on the head and sent her away with none of her questions answered. She dressed appropriately for a ride in jeans and boots, a plaid flannel shirt and a maroon cowgirl hat.

Much as she hated missing a meal, she skipped breakfast and grabbed a ham-and-cheese sandwich for an early lunch before dashing upstairs to the library. The first item on her "to-do" was to find a copy of her dad's published book of poetry and short stories. A slender volume, only one hundred and eighty-five pages, the title was *Lost and Found* by John Joseph Whitman. "Funeral for Fluff-ball" was the third story, a short piece about a beloved friend—a yellow cat with jade green eyes—who never came when called. His description of the journey he made with Dorothy to find the perfect place to set the tombstone was flowery and metaphorical rather than being accurately descriptive. She'd have to be psychic to find Fluffball's grave.

At a few minutes after one o'clock, Simon and Keith entered the library and settled into seats near the sofa. She hooked them both up with mics. After yesterday's emotional session, she was looking forward to a more tangible conversation about how they developed the Simple Simon's franchise.

She asked the most obvious question. "How did you select the name Simple Simon's?"

"Not my idea," Simon said firmly.

"It was marketing," Keith said. "Simon was already building his rep as a chef, and his signature restaurant was Simplicity. We wanted those associations to make people think that this was fast food with a gourmet touch."

"Clever," she said. "Like saying french fries with cheese are potatoes au gratin. Or hamburger is actually Salisbury steak."

"There are significant differences in those recipes."

"Don't get me wrong. I like the names of the dishes on the Simple Simon's menu, and I'm sure you do something different in preparation. They taste better." She'd insulted Keith's cuisine once before, and he hadn't reacted well. This time, her praise was lavish. "I don't know how you make a simple hot dog so delicious."

"The secret is in the sauces and the condiments." Keith flashed his beautiful superwhite smile. "Anything tastes better with gravy or butter or pickled cabbage on the side."

Simon warmed to the topic. When these two partners were talking about food and cooking, they were completely compatible, and Vanessa dutifully recorded it all. The Simple Simon's menu would make a good sidebar for the book, and she wanted to get some of those recipes.

And then she asked, "How did Dorothy feel about the Simple Simon's franchise?"

"She didn't like the idea," Simon said.

"Dorothy considered her husband a culinary genius," Keith said. "She thought it would cheapen his reputation to make his style of cooking available to the masses. It's a good thing we didn't listen to her. Or to any of our wives."

"That's true." Simon bolted to his feet. He'd been sitting still for a long time and needed to vent. "Gloria the supermodel barely eats at all. And Chloe is a nibbler."

"The franchise restaurants have been the big moneymaker, right from the start."

Vanessa headed in a different direction. "I thought you were planning to sell? Didn't Yuri Kirov make an offer?"

"Not yet," Keith said.

"We're considering options," Simon added. "Both of us are thinking about retirement, and Kirov has deep pockets. How about that Macy? There's a woman with a healthy appetite."

"Like a water buffalo," Keith said.

"My Dorothy was like that. She could eat and eat and never gained a pound." He paced around the library. His fiery energy was mostly depleted. "I miss her, can't stop thinking about her. Bethany's murder keeps reminding me."

"The CBI is making progress," Keith said. "They said it was okay for us to go home. The Ingrams are thrilled to pieces. I think they've been missing their game shows on TV. Gloria was almost out of clothes, she's already left for our Aspen condo."

Vanessa caught the hint. She called an end to their session. Her next meeting with Simon wouldn't be for two days. He had other commitments.

As soon as they left, she put away her recording equipment and rushed downstairs, out the door and around the Castle toward the one-story horse barn. She was running a little bit late and was glad to see that Ty had already saddled two horses and was waiting for her. Looking like the archetype of a cowboy sheriff, he sat astride a stallion with a glistening ebony coat. For her, he had saddled a chestnut mare with a floppy mane. Her name was Coco.

Vanessa patted Coco's neck. "Are you ready for me, girl?"

"The guy in the barn said she was your favorite."

"And he was correct." She mounted up. "I'm looking forward to a ride, but it seems odd when we're in the middle of investigating. Why are we doing this?"

"It doesn't seem like there's much else we can do tonight. This afternoon, I tried to dig into court filings and police reports. It was an avalanche of paperwork. Tremont County didn't start digitizing these records until year before last. The filing area contains over a hundred years of paperwork. We're going to have to search on a case-by-case basis."

"An impossible job." Though Vanessa was a research junkie who reveled in organizing documents, this job sounded like too much. "That still doesn't explain why we're on horseback."

"I thought of S&R where I used to work. Much of their information is recorded on maps and GPS. They were happy to help and handed over their file on Aunt Dorothy. Since I have the coordinates, it won't be hard to follow."

"The coordinates to what?" she asked.

"The approximate route Dorothy took on the day of her last ride. We can track her progress from twelve years ago, see where she dismounted from her horse and where her remains were found."

She was impressed with his idea. Following a road into the past might be useful in figuring out what happened. As she flicked her reins and followed him away from the barn, she noticed that he had a rifle tucked into a scabbard on his saddle. The sheriff was prepared for trouble.

Chapter Twelve

Riding single file, they followed a narrow trail through the forest and crested a hill behind the Castle where the landscape spread and flattened into open range and a small herd of cattle grazed. A string of barbed wire separated the dull brown grass from the road that hugged the edge of the foothills to the north. The late afternoon sky was wide open and clear, reminding him of the beautiful desolation of Yellowstone where he grew up. Ty had started riding bareback when he was a little kid, and the rhythm of the stallion's gait felt natural and comfortable.

They were supposed to be investigating a crime, which was serious business, but his mood felt light and cheerful, almost as though he and Vanessa were going on a first date. She nudged forward and pulled even with him. Her brown mare was smaller than his mount, but Coco was more energetic, much like the woman riding her.

Ty sat back in his saddle and watched as she bounced along in her snug jeans and boots. A few wisps of her golden hair slipped out from under the brim of her cowgirl hat and furled against her flushed cheeks. Completely at ease, she smiled broadly.

"Race me," she said, "to that rock on the south side of the meadow that looks like a big fat Buddha."

"You're on, Little Britches."

"Go," she shouted.

He deliberately gave her a couple of seconds head start, not wanting to embarrass her with his superior horsemanship. But she didn't need any favors from him. She leaned forward on Coco and tapped the horse's flanks with her heels They melted into one ferocious entity as Coco stretched forward, showing natural talent as a quarter horse.

Vanessa won by a decent margin and celebrated with a victory whoop and a hug for Coco. With her arms thrust above her head, she used her knees to direct Coco in a circle. The chestnut horse pranced.

"Damn, that feels great!" she shouted. "Let

that be a lesson. Never bet against a Little Britches champion."

"I'll keep that in mind."

"Thanks for suggesting a ride. It feels like we're having too much fun." She pulled herself together. "Okay, I'm settled down. There's work to be done, right? Where are we headed?"

"Farther south to Rattlesnake Ridge."

"How do you know Aunt Dorothy came this way? Are you following a map?"

"I got these directions from word-of-mouth. Before she left the Castle, she told the guy who took care of the horses that she was going to the Ridge. The leader of the S&R team confirmed it."

A popular destination for horseback riders, Rattlesnake Ridge was a high rocky ledge that was just wide enough for two riders side-by-side. It fronted the edge of a forest and offered a wide panorama.

"I know the Ridge," she said. "I like to watch the sunset from there."

"In a couple of hours, it'll be dusk."

He intended to be back at the Castle before nightfall. There wasn't much cover on the open range, and he didn't want to take a chance on being ambushed. Proceeding at a leisurely pace with only the occasional chirping from birds and critters put him in a contemplative mood. His investigation hadn't gathered many facts. It might be time to use imagination. "I wonder," he said, "when Dorothy took this final ride, what was she thinking about?"

"If she was planning suicide, her surroundings would take on heavy-duty importance. At least, that's what the poets would have us believe. Dad was always pondering life's big questions. What happens when you die? Is Heaven real?"

"You think Dorothy had a deep philosophical nature."

Vanessa shrugged. "What can I say? Eccentricity runs in the family."

"Why would such a woman kill herself?"

"I don't think she did. Sure, she was angry, maybe she was replaying an argument with Simon. Or thinking about how she didn't like the Simple Simon's franchise plan."

"Was he upset with her?" Ty considered their marital relationship a possible motive for suicide, even though neither of them believed she killed herself. "Were they the sort of couple who bickered?"

"That's not how I remember them, but I

was only a kid at the time. Simon is a passionate guy who can be as volatile as a volcano, but I don't think he's abusive. And Dorothy could hold her own in a fight." She snapped her fingers. "That reminds me. I found the story Dad wrote about Mr. Fluffball's funeral. It's a sweet little allegory."

An allegory, huh? Ty felt like he'd gone back in time to English class when he had to struggle his way through symbolism and metaphors. "You're going to have to explain."

"The yellow cat with green eyes is a reference to his older sister, Dorothy, who treated him the way a cat treats an owner."

"Ignoring him, tearing up his best shirt, pissing on his shoes."

"I don't think she ever peed on his personal belongings," she said, "but that's the basic gist. Her disdain might even explain the big rift between them twenty years ago."

"How so?"

"My family had weird inheritance traditions. Dorothy got everything. Dad got a cash settlement. He might have resented being cut out."

"And she might have ignored him." That sounded like a motive, but Ty wasn't sure about the crime. "I'd like to see the Fluff-ball story."

"The book is in the library at the Castle."

He directed their horses through a stand of burnished aspen almost turned to gold, then through other trees and foliage until they were on the Ridge, gazing out across miles of acreage. He acted as tour guide. "In the distance to the west, you can see the out-skirts of Greenwell, the population center of Tremont County. And if you follow that road leading away from town, you'll come to the turnoff for my cabin."

"I didn't realize you lived so close to the Castle," she said.

Mountain topography made it difficult to judge distance. A straight line from his cabin to the Castle was probably only seven miles, but when the ups and downs were factored in and the wasted time going around rocks, rivers, trees and hills, those miles doubled or tripled. If he could fly from home to the Castle, the commute would take only a few minutes. "It's quicker to get here on horse-back than to drive."

He dismounted, activated a handheld GPS and fed in the coordinates for the first stop on Dorothy's last ride. He zoomed in on their location. When he'd walked only twenty paces, he hit the spot. "This is where she stopped and got off her horse."

"How can you tell?"

"Check the notation in the S&R worker's book." He reached into the saddlebag and pulled out a computer notebook. "This search team took detailed notes so they could tell where they started and where they left off. In the case of Aunt Dorothy, they had a bunch of volunteers helping."

Vanessa booted up the screen and read the info. "Thirty-two volunteers searched for ten hours on the day after she went missing."

He'd worked on similar Search and Rescue projects. "The assumption in a situation like this is that Dorothy had an accident, maybe her horse got spooked and threw her. Or maybe she got careless and fell."

"How do they find her?"

"The person in charge of the team is usually an expert tracker. He or she studies scuff marks on the ground, broken twigs, footprints and such to determine the direction the lost person went. Their skill set is amazing, better than any satellite photos or GPS or drone."

"S&R uses drones?"

"In the old days, they used to take helicopters to search for lost hikers. Drones can cover twice the area for half the cost. Search and Rescue operation—especially in a high-class resort area like Aspen—have gotten high tech." Again, he consulted the GPS. "Dorothy went this way, down the sloping hill from the Ridge."

"The note says she didn't fall but descended on foot." Vanessa hunkered down to peer over the edge. "Why would she go this way? It's really steep."

"She could have been looking for something. Or could have lost her balance," he suggested. "There's no way of knowing."

"I'm not interested in falling down the hill to follow." She straightened. "Can we pick up her trail at the bottom?"

"That's a plan."

They returned to their horses and mounted, picking their way along the Ridge until they found a safe descent. While she rode, Vanessa skimmed the information in the notebook. "There's a lot of detail about her horse pacing back and forth on the top of the Ridge. The animal didn't appear to be injured."

"But wouldn't slide down the hill," he said. "Smart horse."

"Could the answer to why Dorothy disappeared be that simple? She got separated from her horse?"

It was frustrating to try on so many possibilities and never know for sure, but he was glad to be here, retracing Dorothy's route, rather than being locked up in a dusty file room in the courthouse. At the base of the hill, he dismounted and gave his full attention to the GPS. Dorothy's trail followed a crazy zigzag pattern, moving in a south by southeast direction. "At this point," he explained, "the volunteers would be called upon. They'd spread out in a web, six to ten feet apart, and look for clues."

Vanessa followed him, leading both horses by their reins. "The erratic way she was staggering around makes me think she was drunk or on medication. She might have been ill, suffering from a seizure or passed out. Can we get access to her medical records?"

"Do you know her doctor's name?"

"I don't, but George Ingram might have something in his notes. We should talk to him about cause of death. I'll put the Doc on my to-do list."

Dorothy's stumbling walk came to an end at the edge of a wide ravine.

She scrolled to another screen in the notebook from S&R. "Oh, my God, Ty. Take a look at this."

The screen displayed a photograph. The caption gave the location where it was found by one of the volunteers. The gold locket appeared to be identical to the one he still carried in his pocket with the heart and the arrow circle. "That's proof. We're on the right path."

"But we still don't know what Dorothy was doing out here." She sat on the edge of a table-sized rock and gazed in all directions. "Was she running *toward* something? Or *away* from it? Did the S&R people find indications that she met someone else?"

"Nothing that they made a note about."

As Vanessa turned her thoughts inward, he saw an impressive depth of concentration. She had separated from her aunt at an early age and had lost track of the woman in later life, but Vanessa's connection to her family was bone-deep. She was a Whitman through and through. All the other facts and evidence seemed unimportant compared to her DNA memories. Not that Ty believed in psychic powers, but he could see a connection between Vanessa and the dead woman.

"If I had to guess," she said, "I'd say that Aunt Dorothy was running away from something or someone who followed her to Rattlesnake Ridge. That's why she slid down the steep slope instead of taking the time to find a safer descent. And it's why she was charging around in a crazy pattern. She was trying to escape."

The hairs on the back of Ty's neck prickled. Was Vanessa right? "You think she was being hunted by someone on the Ridge?"

"The big mistake she made was sliding off the Ridge. Her instinct might have been to put distance between herself and her pursuer, but when she was down here on this wide stretch of grassland, there was no cover. She would have been an easy target for a gunman up here on the Ridge. He could sit back and wait until she was in his sites."

Her story was all supposition. No facts. And yet, it made sense. He sat beside her on the rock, almost touching but not quite. Only a whisper of open air—a few inches—separated them. "Where is this vision of the past coming from? You seem to be an organized, down-to-earth woman, like your aunt."

"But I have a wild imagination like Dad. When I get this figured out, I'll let you know." She lightly patted his cheek, then she stood.

"Does the GPS tell you where she went from here?"

He consulted the finder. "From this point, it's direct and simple. She ran that way. Toward Buzzard Creek."

At this time of year, early autumn, there wasn't much water in the creek. It was only a few feet wide. Dorothy had made her dash a few months later in November. The creek bed would have been almost dry.

He followed Vanessa into a wide ravine where a mere trickle splashed in a winding path through shrubs and a clump of cottonwood trees. If Vanessa's imaginings were correct and Dorothy had been trying to escape, this would have been a logical direction. In the ravine, she could take cover and hide from the hunter with a rifle.

On the creek bank, Vanessa stopped walking and allowed Coco to take a drink. "Which way did Dorothy go?"

"Both."

The information shown on his GPS was inconclusive. There were signs that she'd gone one way and then the other. "What does it say in the notes?"

"Pretty much what you said." She scrolled to a new screen. "Nearly a mile upstream, then she doubled back and went twice that far downstream."

And then the big revelation. In his head, Ty played a drumroll. "And then, she vanished. There was no clear indication that she'd left the creek or had linked up with someone on horseback. She was just gone."

Vanessa skimmed the next page in the notebook. "Volunteers went four miles in each direction until it got dark. They found nothing."

"And the next day, it snowed five inches, four more on the day after that."

"The perfect storm," she said. "After the snow and the spring runoff, there wouldn't have been much of a trail for S&R to follow."

"But they didn't give up on Aunt Dorothy. Cops aren't the only ones who are haunted by a cold case they can't solve. Throughout the winter and into the spring, search parties combed this area whenever they had spare time." He watched his handsome stallion approach the creek and disdainfully dip his head to drink. "In March, after the spring thaw, they found her remains in a cave across the river. There was some question about how she'd gotten all the way across the creek and up the hill, but there wasn't much of her left to figure it out. Just a skull, some leg bones and ribs."

"Was there any other evidence?"

"Nada."

He casually stroked the flank of the black stallion and felt a tension under the heavy muscles. The powerful animal jerked his head suddenly as though he'd been startled, and then he looked to the left toward Rattlesnake Ridge. Ty followed the direction of the horse's gaze and saw the glint of sunlight against metal. The barrel of a rifle?

He snatched his weapon from the saddle scabbard and yelled, "Vanessa, get down!"

From the corner of his eye, he saw her dive behind a clump of leafless bushes. Ty slapped his horse on the rump. Didn't want the stallion to be accidentally shot.

Raising his weapon, he aimed toward the spot where he'd seen the reflection.

The other gunman fired first.

Chapter Thirteen

Lying on her belly in the dirt beside the creek, Vanessa froze in panic. The gunfire from Ty's rifle was thunderous. She couldn't tear her gaze away from him. It was obvious that the man knew how to shoot. His standing form was textbook perfection. Then he dropped to one knee and continued.

She believed in him, believed he would do everything he could to protect her. But the echo of returning gunfire terrified her. Someone was shooting at them. They were the targets, the prey. Was this what Aunt Dorothy had felt when a gunman ambushed her and she couldn't escape? Or had she imagined the whole thing and ended the confrontation by taking fate into her own hands and committing suicide?

Ty looked over his shoulder toward her and shouted something. She couldn't understand his words but tried to reassure him by giving an okay signal.

"I'm fine," she said. *Am I?* She didn't think she'd been hit by a bullet but couldn't feel her legs or arms. She checked herself for wounds by wiggling her toes, patting down her body and scanning for blood. A red smear slashed across her upper left arm and her flannel shirt was torn. She'd been grazed by a bullet and hadn't even felt the impact.

"Vanessa!" Ty shouted.

"What?"

He tossed his cell phone in her direction. "Hit the speed dial for Gert in dispatch. I need backup. ASAP. If we're going to catch this guy, we've got to move fast."

With bullets whizzing over her head, Vanessa made the call to Gert Hepple. She'd spoken to the dispatcher a couple of times when she was trying to reach the sheriff to invite him to dinner. *Had that been a hundred years ago?* She recognized the raspy voice of the feisty older woman.

"Sheriff, I'm guessing you've gotten yourself into trouble," Gert said. "What's up?"

"This is Vanessa Whitman. I'm with the sheriff, and he needs backup. Send all the deputies. ASAP."

"How come?"

Seriously? Not the time for a chat. "We're taking gunfire. I've been hit. We're at Buzzard Creek near Rattlesnake Ridge."

Vanessa disconnected the call before Gert could ask more questions she couldn't answer. Vanessa had no idea how she'd *gotten into trouble.* This was a nightmare. She was an English teacher, a ghostwriter for a celebrity chef. Why would someone shoot at her? Who wanted her dead? *Nightmare!* Even the names for the local landmarks were threatening: Rattlesnake Ridge and Buzzard Creek. What else? Grizzly Gulch? Murder Mountain? Wolf Rabies Road? Dad had always encouraged her to be more adventurous, but she was sure this wasn't what he'd had in mind.

Ty lowered his rifle, duck-walked toward her, staying low, and lay down beside her in the dirt. "Are you okay?"

"Been better." She pointed to the blood on her shirt. "I was shot. I think it's just a scratch, but I can't tell."

He tore off her sleeve to study the wound. "Doesn't appear to be serious. The bullet just grazed you, but you might want to put a trip to the emergency room on your to-do list. Otherwise, that might leave a scar."

"What if I want a scar?" What she really wanted was for him to comfort her, to hold her in his arms and stroke her hair. She wanted to thank him for saving her life, but she couldn't let down her guard and be vulnerable. Instead, she snapped and growled. "A gunshot wound might make me into a more interesting person."

"You're plenty interesting." When he leaned close and kissed her forehead, she felt heat radiating from his body. His neck and upper chest glistened with sweat. "I need to ask you for a favor, Vanessa."

"Okay."

"Would you mind if I left you here for a couple of minutes?"

"By myself? Alone? Oh. Hell. No."

"The guy on the Ridge hasn't fired his weapon in over two minutes. He might be making a run for it, and I want to stop him."

Anger flared inside her and burned off her fear and confusion. All her second-guessing was moot. She couldn't believe that Ty would just take off and leave her here at the mercy of a killer. "Aren't your deputies supposed to arrive in a few minutes?"

"We're wasting time," he said. "I won't leave if you need me."

She refused to play the role of wimpy damsel in distress. "I'll come with you."

He looked shocked and surprised. The expression on his face was almost worth the risk she intended to take. Moving stiffly, she stood and dusted the front of her jeans. About a hundred yards away, she saw Coco and Ty's stallion munching on the dull, dry grass in the meadow. When Vanessa whistled and made a clicking noise with her tongue, Coco responded. They'd spent enough time together that they'd developed their own private language. In seconds, the chestnut mare was at her side, impatiently pawing at the dust.

Vanessa handed the phone to Ty. "Looks like your horse isn't coming."

From a distance, she heard police sirens. On the road from town, two patrol cars approached with lights flashing. If the shooter hadn't taken off before now, he was surely on his way.

"He couldn't have gone far." Ty whistled to his horse and waved. The stallion turned his head and looked away. A definite snub. "If we can find the shooter's location, we can determine if he was riding a horse."

"Or an ATV or a motorbike or maybe he parked on the road and hiked." She mounted

Coco. "A more efficient approach to figuring out who was shooting at me would be to focus on the limited number of people in this area who know what we're looking for."

"Limited number?"

There were the eight dinner guests from last night, the staff that worked at the Castle and the chefs in the kitchen. Added to that were the deputies, the cop from Aspen and the CBI agents. "It might be a fairly long list."

"And the shooter could be someone you've never met, like a hired gun. He could be working for the person who wants you dead."

This investigation was more complex than she had anticipated. If she went back in time, she could probably remember another dozen or so people who she'd offended or those who had grudges against the Whitmans. Many people might want to shoot her, but most were sane and didn't act on minor hostility. "Coco and I will ride over and pick up your horse. What's his name? Diablo?"

"He has kind of a bad rep."

"Diablo is perfect."

When she and Coco got closer, Diablo stamped the earth and tossed his head like the demon horse he was. But it only took a small nicker from Coco to calm him. Vanessa took the reins and returned to where Ty was standing with his hat pushed back on his head and his rifle resting on his shoulder. One of the SUV patrol cars had left the road and was driving across the field toward them.

"Here's what we're going to do," Ty said. "You're going to ride into town in a patrol car with Randall. He'll take you to the courthouse, and you'll stay there with Gert. The deputies and I are going to get the horses back to the Castle barn, talk to Agent Morris and do some investigating on our own to see which of our suspects might have been out on the Ridge. Then I'll come back and pick you up."

"I can live with that."

Before he mounted, Ty stroked Diablo's long nose and whispered, "People might call you a demon, but you saved my life. I never would have seen than gunman if you hadn't shown me where he was."

He gave Diablo a kiss. *Lucky horse.*

THE TREMONT COUNTY COURTHOUSE in the middle of Greenwell sat across from the town square with the yellow gazebo. For such a small county, the three-story building was an impressive structure made from the same granite that had been used in building Whitman Castle. Randall escorted Vanessa up the front staircase and held the door to the main floor open for her.

"To your right," he said, "is the formal courtroom with wood pews, desks, a bench for the judge and a carved statue of justice with her blindfold. We don't have enough crime for a full-time magistrate, but we have a traveling judge who sits on Tuesday and Thursday."

She loved the idea of a town so peaceful that they only needed a part-time judge. "Can we take a look inside?"

"Sorry, the courtroom is locked when it's not in use. The same goes for the offices on this floor. All the big shots—the elected mayor of the city and county, the treasurer and the county clerk—have office space, but their hours aren't regular. They all have other jobs." As he strolled on the polished wood floor, his boots made a solid thunk with each step. "Have you ever been in this building before?" he asked.

"Probably when I was a kid. I don't remember."

"Too bad you had to move away."

"Is it?" she asked.

"Growing up in a small town like Greenwell gives you a sense of security and peace. I wouldn't change a thing. I've known some of my neighbors all my life. My wife was my high school girlfriend, and we're starting a new generation with a four-year-old daughter and another on the way. Oops, I'm not supposed to say anything about the new baby. Not yet."

Randall seemed happy and secure. When he said that he *wouldn't change a thing* about his life, she believed him. In a way, she envied the deputy and Ty and all the others who had a confirmed sense of identity. If Dad and Mom had stayed at the Castle and she'd grown up there, she might have been the same way…but probably not. Vanessa liked peace and quiet but needed stimulation. She shared her father's desire for adventure.

Randall took her downstairs to the garden level of the courthouse, which was dedicated to law enforcement. Ty had a separate office. The other deputies had desks in a bullpen arrangement. Directly opposite the entrance, Gert Hepple reigned over the phones, computers and communication systems. The front of her L-shaped desk held the standard in-and out-boxes and forms as well as pens, pencils and markers. There were also jellybeans in a glass jar and a gang of photos. The right side of her L-desk was for her electronic equipment.

As Vanessa approached, Gert leaned back in her swivel chair and observed. A wiry little woman with short red hair that stuck out in all directions like antennae, she wore a telephone headset like it was an accessory. Her fingers drummed on her desktop. When she made eye contact with Vanessa, Gert frowned. They hadn't met before, and Vanessa had no idea why this woman would be hostile toward her.

Gert dismissed Randall and beckoned for Vanessa to come closer. Her thin lips drew into a tight circle. When Vanessa was at the very edge of her desk, Gert said, "I was sorry to hear about your father. It was cancer, right?"

"It was." And not something she wanted to discuss in detail. Vanessa had heard a lot of cancer stories, and few of them had happy endings. "Thank you for your condolences."

"Buried in Denver?"

Odd question. This was the first time anyone had asked about Dad's final resting place. "Cremated. I spread some of his ashes at my mother's grave site. He wanted another portion to be spread in the mountains, but I haven't figured out the right place."

"Well, that's easy." Gert said. "He ought to be buried next to Dorothy."

As soon as Gert made her suggestion, Vanessa knew that was the answer she was looking for. Dad didn't care about the Castle or the Whitman properties. Though he and his sister were estranged, he needed to be with her. "Do you know where Dorothy is buried?"

"Nope." Gert unplugged her headset and came out from her desk fortress. "Simon had a big memorial service at the Chapel on the Hill before her body was found, and everybody attended. Afterward, we went to the Castle and had a full buffet dinner. Best prime rib I ever tasted. Say what you want about Simon Markham, but the man knows how to cook."

Vanessa knew that the best way to mine gold nuggets from a gossip was to sit back and let her talk. Sooner or later, something interesting would appear. But there wasn't time to sit and listen for hours on end…not while somebody was shooting at her. "I like your idea about scattering Dad near his sister. Would the local pastor know her burial spot?"

"Give me a minute and I'll call him. Do you want coffee?"

Vanessa was certain that the brew from the coffee machine in the kitchenette would be an insult to the incredible blend she was served at the Castle, but it would be rude to refuse. "Thanks, I'll pour my own."

When they returned to Gert's desk, the dispatcher plugged in her headset and tapped in the numbers for the Chapel on the Hill. Her conversation with the pastor took only a moment, then she turned to Vanessa. "He doesn't know, but I'll keep looking."

Vanessa took a swig of the purely awful coffee. Gert was on her side. Finally, she'd made a friend. "What can you tell me about the police investigation into Dorothy's disappearance?"

"First, I want to hear something from you, missy. I heard that your cousin, Bethany, was having an affair. True or false?"

"Agent Morris wouldn't want me to tell you this—" she saw Gert's eyes brighten in anticipation "—but the answer is yes. Bethany had a lover, and they'd been together for a long time. The affair might have started when she was still in Los Angeles."

Gert leaned forward, anxious for more. "Then it's not that Russian guy, Yuri Kirov?"

"I didn't say that. Yuri is her husband's client, which means Bethany might have known him for a long time. Have you met Yuri and Macy?"

Gert snorted. "We don't exactly run in the same social circles."

"You'd like Macy. She's colorful."

From his desk, Randall called out, "Don't tell her anything else, Vanessa. Not unless you want your business broadcast all over the county."

Gert chided him. "Nobody wants to hear your opinion, Randall. By the way, tell your wife congratulations on the new baby."

"How did you know?"

"I have my sources."

Vanessa was glad to hear that Gert was well connected. The town gossip was precisely the person she needed. Why sort through boxes of files when she could get the information firsthand? She held the coffee mug to her lips but didn't drink. "I heard there were some issues about Dorothy's will and her insurance payments."

"Nothing from insurance." Gert lowered

her voice to a confidential whisper. "It was a suicide, bless her soul."

"Did you happen to know her lawyer? Was he a local?"

"What kind of game are you playing?" Gert's scowl returned with a vengeance. "She had the same lawyer as your father. The Greenwell Law Firm has been handling the personal affairs for the Whitman family for years and years."

During the past four years while she struggled to tried to get her father's life in order, she'd met a circus parade of attorneys and accountants. Lion tamers worked with the IRS. Jugglers tried to balance the artwork and sculpture. And there were many, many clowns. "I don't specifically recall anybody with Greenwell."

"I have their phone number." Gert turned away from her to answer an actual 911 call from a woman with a brown bear loose in her backyard.

Vanessa sat quietly, not drinking coffee and feeling tired. Dusk darkened the skies outside the windows. Where was Ty? He'd bcen gone for over an hour, plenty of time to drive to the Castle and back.

And when he picked her up, where would

she go? It didn't seem safe to return to the Castle when there was a shooter after her. She'd managed to push the threat from her mind, but when she closed her eyes, the sense of danger returned. She remembered the roar of gunfire. When the bullets hit the ground near her, they kicked up a spray of loose dirt.

Gert drummed her fingers on the desktop. "You're tired."

"Did you take care of the bear?"

"I sent Randall to handle the wildlife. He's a good boy, but I'd never tell him. I like to tease." She unplugged her headset. "You're coming with me, young lady. There's a sofa in Ty's office, and I think you need a lie-down."

"I'm fine. My wound is barely a scratch."

"I understand," Gert said. "And the hospital is a long distance away from here. All you need is a little nap."

Vanessa wanted to object, but the gray plaid sofa in Ty's office looked too cozy. By the time she stretched out and wiggled into a comfortable position, she was halfway asleep.

Chapter Fourteen

When Vanessa opened her eyes, she felt like only a few minutes had passed but knew it was longer because the sun had gone down. Outside the windows, it was night and rainy. Someone had covered her with a knitted blue blanket. She swung her legs off the sofa and dropped her feet to the carpeted floor. Her boots were gone, but she was wearing socks.

She stood on wobbly legs, trying to catch her balance. From the doorway, Ty observed her progress. His arms were folded across his chest, and he wore a hooded sweatshirt over his uniform shirt. "About time you woke up," he said.

"Hey, it's the other way around. I've been waiting for you." The outer wall of his office was half glass. She could see the deputy bullpen where the lights were on. In Ty's office, it was dark with only one lamp on the desk shedding a circle of light. Her eyelids drooped but she refused to fade into sleep. "Did you catch him?"

"Not yet."

Her hopes crashed. Somewhere out there in the rainy night was both the shooter who tried to kill her and the stalker. She wanted to believe they were the same individual but didn't know, not for sure. There could be a dozen thugs in black ski masks who were after her. "Do you know who it is?"

"It's not Simon. He was at a meeting with a DEA agent, unrelated to the murder. And it's not Chloe or Gloria Gable who were both shopping in Aspen. None of the others have alibis. As soon as Agent Morris told the suspects that they could go home, they scattered."

"He makes a mistake, and I'm the one who pays for it." She collapsed onto the sofa again. "Are they at least looking?"

"Morris is putting in every effort. In addition to his team from CBI, he's called out the Aspen police and the state patrol."

Ty sat beside her, and she leaned against his shoulder. She pinched a piece of the soft fabric of his sweatshirt. It was dry. "You haven't been out in the rain," she said.

"I wanted to get back here as fast as possible."

"Tell me about the searchers. What did they find?"

"The forensic experts went to Rattlesnake Ridge. They found tire tracks that looked like an off-road vehicle and footprints, nothing unusual about either. There were plenty of shell casings. If we ever find his rifle, we can make a ballistic match." He slipped his arm around her shoulder and squeezed. "Then it started raining."

"And the evidence was washed away."

"The investigation is ongoing. State patrol is checking traffic cams and going through registration for vehicles in the area. Cops and other agents are verifying alibis."

She was sure that everybody was doing their best, but she doubted they'd find the shooter. The search was futile. Everything was futile. Her eyes closed.

"Don't fall asleep." He nudged her. "Do you need a trip to the hospital?"

"It's in Aspen, forty-five minutes away."

"We need to get you home to bed."

"Not the Castle." A ripple of fear rolled up and down her spine. "I won't be able to sleep there."

He pulled her close. "Rough day."

"Intense." Her mind drifted. She remembered lying in the dirt beside a creek while gunfire erupted. The booming echoed inside her head. *A shooter tried to kill me.* They had been following the path of a dead woman. Twelve years ago, Aunt Dorothy's remains had been torn apart by predators.

She leaned against Ty, burrowed into his broad chest. A sharp pain stabbed her upper left arm, and she remembered. "I was shot."

"I know." His voice was as soothing as a caress. "We talked about your wound, put it on your to-do list."

"Do you think I need stitches?"

"It's up to you."

"I'll probably have to get stitches."

She really needed to make a new list. There were so many things to do. "I need to go to Greenwell Law Firm," she mumbled. "And I want to find out from Simon where Dorothy is buried."

"Whatever you need to do, we'll take care of it."

She remembered the sweet chestnut mare she'd been riding. "What about Coco? Did you get her back to the horse barn?"

"She's at home in her stall, nibbling hay. I made sure she had an apple for a treat."

She curled her legs and cuddled more tightly against him. "About those stitches… I don't want to go to a hospital."

"I thought you might feel that way," he said. "I brought the doctor to you. Look out the window toward Gert's desk."

Though she hated to leave the comfort of his arms, she twisted around and stared. Doc Ingram and his wife, Martha, were talking to Gert. Actually, the two women were chuckling and chattering while Doc silently swilled coffee from a mug.

"Coffee." She scowled like a kid who had been served a plateful of broccoli. "That brew is miserable, but I need caffeine."

"Gert's lousy coffee is legendary, so Martha brought a fresh bag of dark roast. Are you ready to get sewn up?"

"Coffee first."

That should provide the motivation she needed. In her stocking feet, she padded across the office to Gert's desk, greeted everybody and went to the kitchenette where the coffee maker awaited. She filled a mug half-full, sniffed and took a sip. Not gourmet but good enough.

Doc Ingram carried his old-fashioned doctor bag into the kitchenette/break room. Martha accompanied them. While she told Vanessa that she was being very brave, she swabbed down one of the tables and laid out paper towels.

Doc washed his hands. "Thank you, Martha."

"I like being your nurse." She went up on tiptoe to kiss his cheek.

He sent her on her way and turned to Vanessa. "Sit here, roll up your sleeve and let me take a look at that gunshot wound."

"I never thought I'd hear someone say that to me. A gunshot wound? Me?"

"Your life is far more exciting than you think it is. After all, you're a Whitman."

"What's that supposed to mean?"

"You're entitled to be eccentric."

As he inspected her arm, she realized that she hadn't exchanged more than a dozen words with George Ingram. In the first go-around of interviews, he wasn't high on her list of witnesses, partly because he didn't fit her expectations for Bethany's lover; also Martha kept him on a short leash. And he was intoxicated for most of the evening. Not that an alcoholic couldn't pull off a complicated murder. But Doc Ingram wasn't a peppy drunk. He seemed to be perpetually on the edge of falling asleep.

Using water from the sink, he cleaned her wound. "If you're concerned about scarring, I'd advise you to seek treatment from a specialist. I can recommend a plastic surgeon in Aspen."

She shrugged her shoulders. "I'm only concerned about avoiding infection."

"Does it hurt?" he asked. "On a scale from one to ten, how painful?"

She'd been through this exercise a million times with Dad and his docs. If she registered from two to five, she'd get over-the-counter pain relief. Seven and above moved her into the morphine range. She diagnosed herself. "I want something to take the edge off, but I need to stay alert. You know, in case somebody tries to kill me again."

When he smiled, she caught a glimpse of the man Martha had fallen in love with—the man she called a silver fox. "I never really knew your father," he said. "But you remind me of Dorothy."

"Why is that?"

"You're smart and pretty." He assembled the tools of his trade, including antiseptic, butterfly bandages, thread and a hypodermic. "You're going to feel a pinch. That's the local anesthetic to dull the area where I'm stitching."

"Her death was a tragedy."

"Tragic." Sitting beside her, he administered the hypodermic so skillfully that she barely felt the needle. "Telling Simon that his wife committed suicide was one of the hardest things I've ever done. Their marriage wasn't perfect, but he loved her deeply."

She believed him. Why else would Simon turn his late wife's sewing room into a shrine?

"Also," Doc said, "I was going through a difficult time when Dorothy disappeared. Vision problems. For a while, I thought I might go blind, nearly drove poor Martha crazy. But I had a couple of successful surgeries, and I recovered."

"You were lucky."

He whispered in her ear, "I also had a prescription for medical marijuana."

"Don't worry, Doc. It's legal." She remembered Ty telling her that Simon was talking to a DEA agent. About drugs? Doc's grandson who lived with them might be involved with a drug dealer at Simplicity. "I'm sure you keep your, um, stash locked up."

"You bet. If my grandson got his paws on my pot, that would be a problem. Is your arm numb?" She nodded, and he turned his full attention to her wound. As he worked on the stitches, he moved her arm to different angles in order to study his handiwork. In a few quick minutes, he announced, "Done. Seven stitches. If you want, we can get a mirror from Gert so you can see how it turned out."

"It's okay. I trust you."

"You're the kind of easy-going patient I'd want if I were still in practice. But that's not happening, not anymore. I let my medical license lapse."

Good idea. Though Doc had a certain charm, he also had physical problems, drank too much and tried to manage his health issues with pot. And his relationship with Martha was puzzling. There had to be a reason his wife didn't let him out of her sight.

Vanessa wanted to believe that he'd been a good doctor for most of his career. As long as he fulfilled his oath to *do no harm*, he deserved a happy retirement. "Here's the deal, Doc. All you need to worry about is relaxing and finding the next great fishing hole."

"But I like staying involved as coroner. No

pressure. My patients are dead, and I can't hurt them."

He reached into his shirt pocket and pulled out a slender instrument. He removed the cover. "What's that?" she asked.

"My lucky scalpel." He pulled off the cover, revealing a sharp blade, which he used to cut the thread. "I like to carry it with me. Reminds me that I'm still a doctor."

"Do you miss being a doctor?"

"Sometimes." He handled the scalpel deftly, then he wrapped her arm in a tidy bandage and gave her instructions about applying antiseptic and not getting the wound dirty. "You're all done."

"Thanks, Doc." He really did have a kind smile. "Do you mind if I ask you a question not related to the stitches?"

"Shoot!" He mimed a quick draw and chuckled at his own joke.

"I want to pay my respects to Dorothy. Do you know where her remains are buried?"

"I thought you knew." He cocked his head to one side and studied her suspiciously. "In fact, I reckoned that you were the only living person who knew."

"Why would you think that?"

"Dorothy had a stipulation in her will.

She wanted your father to bury her in whatever manner he saw fit in whatever grave he thought appropriate."

Vanessa took a moment to absorb this information, and listened intently as the doctor continued to talk. There was something very strange about the Whitman family and burial places. Dad wanted a three-stage scattering of ashes, and Dorothy had recruited her estranged brother for the task. What had Dad done with Dorothy? She thought of his ashes in the urn in the Castle library, and she could almost hear him laughing.

AT TEN THIRTY, it wasn't raining hard, but Ty needed an umbrella when he escorted her out of the courthouse and into his SUV patrol car. He didn't know where he should take her, but she was determined *not* to spend the night at the Castle.

A fierce display of static lightning slashed across the night sky. Thunder followed. Electric storms weren't unusual in Colorado, but they felt like a phenomenon and often resulted in disasters like forest fires.

He and Vanessa shivered inside his SUV. The humidity was out of whack for the arid mountain climate. He started the engine. "I picked up some of your clothes and stuff when I was at the Castle. Ought to be enough for tonight. Where should I take you? A motel?"

"I don't want to be alone," she said. "Not that I'm scared, but I might need protection."

"We could go to my cabin. I've been renovating it in my spare time."

He gritted his teeth, wanting to bite back his words and swallow them. His relationship with Vanessa was complicated. He thought she was sexy and desirable in every way, but they weren't dating, and he didn't want to push too hard.

"I could go to your place," she said. "You mentioned renovations, and I'd like to see what you've done."

She wanted to discuss home-improvement projects? Not what he had in mind when he thought of an evening alone with her. "Don't get excited. I've got lots more projects."

"You're kind of a nester, aren't you? Like a bird that gathers bits of straw and fabric to build a perfect nest for the eggs."

"Back it up," he said. "I'm not interested in eggs."

"You don't think you are, but eggs are the entire purpose of a nest. It's a place for the fledglings to hang out before they learn to fly."

That was a very disturbing metaphor. Simile? Allegory? To avoid thinking about nesting, he concentrated on the road. The route to his house was easy, requiring only two right turns before veering onto three miles of winding road through a pine forest. Lightning flashed again, setting fire to the skies. "Don't all birds make nests?"

"I guess. But some birds have fun first. They migrate from the Aleutian Islands to Guadalajara, flying hundreds of miles for a change of scenery."

"Are you an exotic migrator?"

"I don't know. Sometimes, I long for the security of the nest. Other times, I want to fly like Dad." She fluttered her arm. "Speaking of Dad…"

Now what? "Go on."

"I asked Doc if he could tell me where Dorothy was buried. And he was shocked that I didn't know." Her lips curved in a sly smile. "In her will, Dorothy appointed my father to handle her final remains—a responsibility that most people would think meant dealing with cemeteries and funeral services."

Inwardly, Ty groaned. "I'm guessing that your dad went a different route."

"There had already been a memorial service, a few months before they found Dorothy, so it didn't seem right to do that again. And Simon was devastated by the fact that she'd killed herself. I don't think he meant to keep the suicide a secret, but he didn't want to talk about it."

Ty understood. This was a gossipy little area, and the Whitman family was a big deal. With Gert leading the charge, Simon would have to explain again and again what he might have said to set his wife off. "What did your father do?"

"He showed up at the Castle. Simon was too upset to deal with him. It was left to Doc and Keith to hand over the airtight metal box that held Dorothy's remains."

"Not a coffin?"

"After Doc cleaned up the pieces of Aunt Dorothy, there wasn't much left to bury—a skull and a couple of bones. Dad put the box that was about the size of an ice chest on a gurney, wheeled it out to his van and drove away. He never told anyone where he went."

Outside, the lightning sizzled, which suited

the mood of this morbid story. Ty wrapped it up. "Doc thought he must have told you."

"A logical conclusion. Mom was dead and buried. I wasn't aware of any close friends Dorothy might have had." She adjusted her position in the passenger seat so she didn't put weight on her injured arm. "We need to find Dorothy's burial site and excavate that box."

"God help me, I agree." Every time they raked up a new chunk of evidence, Aunt Dorothy's cold case took on more significance. "The metal box is suspicious. I want to know what's inside."

"Dad might have left a clue about where she was buried in the Fluffball story."

"I found your father's book in the library," he said. "I stuck it in your backpack."

"It'll make a great bedtime story."

The final turn on the narrow road that led to his two-story stripped log cabin dodged through a thick stand of ponderosa pine and random boulders. Someday, he wanted to rent a backhoe and clear the rocks. The main work he'd done on the exterior involved repairs to the A-frame roof that peaked over the front entrance. Inside, he'd refinished floors, painted walls and replaced some ancient plumbing fixtures. He enjoyed the work he'd done and was proud of the results, which made him wonder if Vanessa was right about his identity as a domestic nester waiting for eggs.

When she stepped through the front door, she admired his refinished floor and choice of paint using knowledgeable terminology. No stranger to DIY projects, she even identified the color in the dining area as Heather Mist.

"You know what you're talking about," he said. "I'm guessing you've done some of your own renovations."

"I want to be exotic and fly free over Buenos Aires." She wrinkled her nose. "But I'm a nester at heart."

"I like that about you."

Their gazes met, and he was tempted to get close, to inhale the fragrance of her hair, to embrace her and carry her off to his bed. A rumble of thunder encouraged him to take action. Move to the next level. She'd kissed him first on the Hag Stone, opening the door. He wanted to believe it was time to deepen their connection.

In a tiny voice, she asked, "Are we safe here?"

There was no way in hell that he'd put her in danger again. "Even if the bad guy figured out you were here, My cabin has a top-notch security system and I asked two of my deputies to keep watch."

She took a tentative step toward the staircase. "I need to take a shower. Is the bathroom upstairs?"

The rain sluiced down the log cabin walls. The static lightning crackled outside the windows, and thunder roared. A rattling noise came from upstairs. Vanessa gasped. The mood was broken.

"What was that?" she asked.

"A shutter must have torn loose." He charged up the staircase, two at a time. "I'd better take care of that before it blows off. Take the first room to the left. That's the guest room and there's a bathroom attached."

"Thanks for everything," she called after him.

The night wasn't over. More could happen.

Chapter Fifteen

Vanessa rubbed a fluffy yellow towel over her hair and ran a comb through the tangled strands. There was nothing like a steamy hot shower to help you relax. The tension knots at the base of her neck had loosened. Her breath came more easily. Unfortunately, she couldn't snuggle under the slate blue comforter and go to sleep.

The bandage covering her stitched wound had gotten wet, and she needed Ty's help to replace the dressing. Doc had given her antiseptic, gauze pads and bandages. She popped a pain reliever, gathered the necessary supplies and went downstairs.

She found Ty in the small kitchen. His spiky hair was wet, and he'd changed into a maroon University of Montana T-shirt. She pointed to the bear claw "Griz" logo. "Did you go to college there?"

"Played football for a couple of years. Go Grizzlies! Then I busted my leg." His hand automatically dropped to his thigh, muscle memory of an injury. "Never made it back to school."

"I'm sorry."

"Don't be," he said. "That winter I came to Aspen and started teaching skiing."

"I'm guessing that was against medical advice."

"Not really," he said. "The docs said I should exercise to rehabilitate my leg. Teaching kids to ski isn't heavy duty. By the next season, I was on the ski patrol."

She noticed a tea setting with two cups and a china teapot on the kitchen table. There was also a plate of cookies. "Midnight snack?"

"I figured you'd need to change the dressing on your arm, and a cup of chamomile might help us both get to sleep."

Ty was a nice guy, but this level of thoughtful behavior was above and beyond. He couldn't possibly have an adorable teapot with pattern of butterflies and rosebuds ready for immediate use. He must have searched his cabinets for it.

He pulled out a chair for her at the table. How could this guy who played football for the Grizzlies be so sweet? Her thoughts drifted toward the memory of their kiss, which had been gentle and controlled. When they kissed again, would there be passion? She hoped so. Vanessa was ready to be swept away on an exotic adventure.

Filling their teacups, adding honey and stirring felt like an old-fashioned version of foreplay. So many Regency romances—one of her favorite choices for recreational reading—were full of repressed desire and tea drinking. She gazed at him over the rim of her cup. Could this Colorado sheriff be her modern version of Mr. Darcy?

He placed a small notebook and a pen by her elbow. "I thought you might want to make a list for tomorrow."

He was absolutely correct. Listing her responsibilities would clear her mind and help her think about something other than the shape of his mouth and the deep green undertones in his gray eyes. She picked up the pen and tapped it on the tabletop. She didn't have a session with Simon on her agenda. Though she could always work on transcription, it wasn't an urgent task.

"Headings," she said. "Number one is Aunt Dorothy's remains. We need to find her burial site, dig up the metal box and see what's inside. What do you think it looks like?"

"An ice chest or mini-fridge." He drained his teacup in a manly gulp and poured another with the delicate touch of a Regency gentleman. "Here's what we're not going to do—wander around the open range making targets of ourselves. We need to limit the search area."

"We should study the Fluffball story for mention of a landmark." She made a short-hand note on her list. "And check the photo of Dad and Dorothy as kids."

"And when we find that landmark, I have an idea of how to search without revealing ourselves to the bad guy."

"How?"

"We have access to technology that wasn't available when Dorothy first disappeared." He paused for effect and snapped his fingers. "Drones."

"I'm impressed. Do you have a drone?"

"S&R has several. We'll determine a limited area and search for the cat's gravestone."

"That's brilliant! I could kiss you."

"Could you?" His voice dropped to a low sexy baritone. "I wouldn't stop you."

She was tempted yet held back. "Next item

on the list—paperwork. Gert mentioned the Greenwell Law Firm handled some of the Whitman family business."

"What do you think you'll learn from them?"

So many of the twists and turns of her family's relationship were tangled with wills, ownership documents and insurance policies. Thoughtfully, she nibbled on a chocolate cookie and sipped her tea. "I don't know, but it's worth a visit to the law firm. Also, these legal papers circle back to Bethany's murder."

"I have an item for your list," he said. "Agent Morris wants to do a reenactment figuring out where everybody was at the time of the murder. That's not for tomorrow but the next day."

"Why do we have to be there? We're not suspects."

"Witnesses," he said. "We retrace our route, and maybe we'll remember something significant."

She made a note. "We should probably stop at the Castle tomorrow. Morris might have information on the autopsy. After we search with the drone, we'll stop by. That makes it a full day. We should start early tomorrow morning."

"Yes, ma'am," he drawled. "Let me replace that bandage."

He went to the sink to wash his hands before he pulled his chair around to sit beside her, much the way Doc had done. Ty's medical expertise was evident in the way he gently but firmly handled her wounded arm, but his touch had a special quality. When he pushed aside the short sleeve of her lightweight flannel pajamas and his hand brushed her bare arm, goose bumps prickled across her skin.

"How does it look?" she asked.

"Doc did a good job with the stitches." He dabbed antiseptic on the wound and blew on it so it would dry quickly. His breath was cool and soothing. "You won't have much of a scar."

He carefully replaced the dressing and bandage. It felt like such a small wound didn't deserve all this attention, but she appreciated the care. "I've never been shot before."

"Let's hope this is the last time." He glided the tip of his finger down her arm from her shoulder to her wrist. "That bandage ought to last until the next shower."

She turned her head and studied the expression on his face. "You're good at taking care of people. And you're a nester. Why don't you have a girlfriend?"

"You sound like my mother."

That definitely wasn't the connection she'd hoped for. "You're looking forward to settling down, aren't you?"

He took her hand in his. "I'm not like you, Vanessa. I don't make lists and cross off every item. My life isn't well planned. Sometimes, it's confusing. I don't have a girlfriend because I can't go to the Significant Other Shop and pick one up like a loaf of bread. When it's the right time, I'll meet her. The decision will be spontaneous."

"An adventure," she said. "When do you think you'll meet her?"

"Maybe I already have."

Let it be me. "On the Hag Stone, I kissed you first. We've had a couple little nudges and hugs, but I'm waiting for serious payback."

Still holding her hand, he stood and tugged her closer. "How serious?"

"A definite kiss, the kind that makes my toes curl and my eyeballs roll back in my head."

His mouth joined with hers. The pressure felt just right—not ferocious and not mushy. His lips teased. It was sensual magic. His tongue penetrated her mouth and tangled with hers.

She pressed her body against his, melting into him, feeling every possible sensation. At the same time, she went into a dream state where she couldn't tell hard from soft, hot from cold, up from down. Her mention of toe curling wasn't far off the mark. His kiss made her feel like she was floating on air.

It had been a long time since she'd been with a man. Were they moving too fast? She didn't want to hurt Ty or lead him on. Vanessa was almost thirty, not an easily excited teenager. She needed to be responsible. With an effort, she forced herself to separate from him. The space between them felt like an Arctic abyss.

Breathing hard, she said, "I don't want you to get the wrong idea."

"We're on the same page," he said. "We both want to go upstairs and slide between the sheets. I want you in my bed, lying beside me, naked."

"Yes, I want that, too." *Be responsible.* "But there's no promise of anything more than tonight, one night. We're not going to build a nest together. Do you understand?"

He gazed at her with such flaming intensity that she actually felt her temperature rise. "This has got to be the most formal declaration of casual sex I've ever heard. I'm not asking for a commitment, Vanessa. Any time you feel like we should stop, I'll back off. No hard feelings."

"I like you, Ty. I don't want to hurt you."

"I'm a grown man. I can take care of myself."

He proved that point by unbuttoning her pajama top and slipping his hand inside. He slung his other arm around her waist and yanked her against him. She couldn't resist, didn't want to. Instead, she kissed him again, and she reveled in his touch. He fondled her in a full-body caress, paying particular attention to her breasts. His hands slid down her torso until he cupped her bottom. He squeezed and held her against him.

Outside, the lightning had subsided, but the rain continued to spill down the windows. She couldn't see more than a few feet into the darkness, but a watcher could peer into Ty's cabin. She felt exposed. The stalker might be nearby. Two deputies were keeping an eye on them. She didn't want to put on a show.

"Your bed." She gasped. "Upstairs. Now."

Tangled together, they stumbled to the

staircase. Ungracefully, they made it to the top, across the landing and into his bedroom, which was twice as large as the guest room. When he reached for the light switch, she slapped his hand away.

"I like the dark," she said.

"I can live with that." He scooped her off her feet and carried her the last few paces to the bed. "I don't want you to trip over something and stumble."

Vanessa was a feminist through and through, but she enjoyed being manhandled, knowing that Ty could lift her and carry her without showing any sign of exertion. In spite of his sensitivity and his dainty teapot, he was a manly man.

In seconds, they were undressed. Under the crisp, cool sheets, their naked bodies curled against each other. In perfect harmony, they made love. They were good together—too good for this to be a mistake.

THE NEXT MORNING, Vanessa woke in a strange bed—Ty's bed. Naked and very happy, she reached toward his side, expecting to touch his broad, muscular shoulder or to drag her fingers through his short bristly hair. He wasn't there. She opened her eyes and stared at the empty pillow. Had last night actually happened? Had she made love—twice—with the handsome, sensitive sheriff of Tremont County?

Sunlight poured through his bay windows. She glanced at the bedside clock and saw that it was almost nine o'clock. She should have been awake an hour ago. They had an agenda. "Ty?"

The center windows were open, and she heard hammering from outside. "Ty?"

"Out here."

She wrapped herself in the comforter to cover her nudity and went to the window. He stood on the peak of the A-frame over the front door, wearing his tool belt, jeans, cowboy hat and nothing else. Bare-chested with the morning sun highlighting the ridges and shadows of his muscular torso, he reminded her of a classical statue. But Ty was better than a marble replica because he was warm and supple. When he took off his hat and grinned, she couldn't believe she'd resisted him for even one minute.

"What are you doing?" she asked.

"Last night when that shutter blew off, it messed up some of the shingles. This is a new roof. I wanted to repair it right away."

Nesting. That was his nature, and he couldn't help himself. "I'm going to call the lawyers and see if we can make an appointment."

"Wait." In his bare feet, he climbed up the shingles to the window, leaned inside and kissed her. "You look beautiful in the morning."

"So do you."

This was a memory she'd treasure forever. Even if their passion was only a one-night affair, she would always remember the vision of a half-naked cowboy outside her window.

Chapter Sixteen

The town of Greenwell wasn't the place where Ty had been born and raised but was so similar that he felt like he'd never left home. The Greenwell town square showed off indigenous landscaping provided by the Garden Society. In the center was a yellow gazebo where the high school jazz combo performed every Sunday evening in the summer. Third Avenue and the attached parking lot separated the Tremont County Courthouse from the square. Most of the businesses lined Main Street, which was to the right of the courthouse. There was slanted parking at the curb and four-way stop signs on each end. No stoplights. On the far corner of Main was Charlie's Diner. That was where Ty took Vanessa for breakfast.

Earlier, she'd called Greenwell Law Firm and managed to set up an appointment for eleven o'clock—about an hour from now. As soon as they took their seats in a burgundy booth near the window, the peppy little waitress Darlene rushed over with a mug of coffee exactly the way he liked it: strong and black. He introduced her to Vanessa.

Darlene's big blue eyes got wide. "You're a Whitman?"

"Grew up in the Castle," Ty informed her.

"Are you related to the woman who got murdered?"

"She was a distant cousin," Vanessa said. "We didn't know each other well."

"Her hubby comes in here all the time, which I think is nuts. He could be eating that fancy gourmet food at the Castle, but he goes for Charlie's greasy burgers and fries."

"Does he meet anybody?" Ty asked.

"Keith Gable and his supermodel wife who never actually eats anything at all. Once I saw Burke with Doc Ingram."

She pivoted and asked Vanessa, "How do you take your coffee?"

"With milk. What's good for breakfast?"

"Bacon and cheesy grits with a fried egg, over-easy."

"I'll have that," Vanessa said.

Ty echoed her order. "With two eggs. Double the bacon and keep the coffee coming."

"You got it, Sheriff."

He gazed across the table at Vanessa—a genuine Whitman. Many small western towns had a family or families who owned the most acreage or ran the greatest number of cattle. They were usually among the first settlers, and people thought of them as royalty. Everybody knew who they were but didn't treat them special, and these frontier aristocrats didn't put on airs.

He asked, "When you were growing up, did you know your family was wealthy?"

"I lived in a castle, Ty. Of course I knew. And I hated being different. Other kids used to pick on me, and I usually started the school year with a couple of good fights."

"You were a tomboy." And he wasn't surprised.

"I just wanted to fit in." She picked up the coffee mug that Darlene had silently delivered with a small pitcher of milk. "It's funny that you should mention the old days. I recognized the name of the lawyer we're going to meet at Greenwell Law Firm. He's Denny Nussbaum. I went to school with him."

She looked down into her coffee, and he

recognized her ploy. When she didn't want to talk about something, she stared off into the distance or blinked or did something else to avoid eye contact. The more he knew about her, the more he liked her. But this time, he wouldn't let her off the hook. "What happened between you and Denny?"

"He was an undersized kid with skinny arms and slouchy posture. And then, there were his ears." She shook her head. "Big floppy ears. He got bullied. The bigger boys called him Denny Dumbo."

Everybody knew someone like Denny. Ty considered it sweet revenge when those who were bullied achieved success. "Now he's a lawyer. Good for him."

"We could have been close friends," she said, "but something happened. I was walking home from school and I saw two boys beating Denny up. I was so mad. I jumped into the middle of their fight and punched the other boys. I knocked one of them down, and he got a bad scrape on his elbow. The other ran off."

"You rescued Denny."

"And you'd think he'd be my friend. We had other stuff in common, like being smart and getting good grades, but he pushed me away. The pendulum swung in the other direction. He told me he didn't need a girl to fight his battles. We hardly talked after that."

Kids sucked. In spite of the good manners his grandma taught him, Ty rested his elbows on the table and reached across to hold Vanessa's hands. This morning, her hair was neatly pulled back and twisted into a bun, which she probably thought was appropriate for meeting a lawyer. She wore pink lipstick, and he thought she was beautiful. "You did the right thing."

Darlene dropped off their eggs and grits and waited until they took a bite so they could tell her the food was delish.

"As good as the stuff they serve at the Castle," Vanessa said.

Darlene winked at the guy working the grill and turned back to Vanessa. "You just made his day."

While they ate, she pulled out the copy of her dad's book with the story of Fluffball's funeral and read highlighted passages. "This part refers to a rock formation that looks like Stonehenge. Does that sound like any of the local landmarks?"

"I can't think of anything," he said. "Did

you bring that photograph with your father and Aunt Dorothy as kids?"

She'd tucked the picture between the pages of the book, a faded Polaroid. As he dug into the cheesy grits, he studied the landscape in the background—pine, aspen and potentilla shrubs with yellow flowers. This photo could have been taken anywhere.

"It can't be too far from the Castle," she said. "Dad and Dorothy were just kids, probably eight and eleven, not strong enough to lug a makeshift coffin any great distance."

"And the paint." As sheriff, he'd had experience with kids marking up the rocks with graffiti. Some of the acrylic paint they used to decorate the tombstone was impossible to get off. "They would have carried the paint."

She lifted a strip of bacon to her lips. "They could have painted the grave marker before they set out to bury the cat."

"But then they'd have to transport the heavy stone."

From careful study of the photo, he guessed that her dad and Dorothy hiked until they found a rock that resembled a gravestone. They painted the edge a bright yellow with blue flowers. In the center, they wrote in black *Mr. Fluffball. Silly cat. Rest in peace.*

"In the story," she said, "Dad described their funeral procession. Both kids had backpacks, which is where they could have put the paint. Dad carried a spade on his shoulder. Dorothy dragged the coffin behind her on a travois."

"Like the Arapaho used to transport their goods and tepees."

"Oh, yeah." She nodded. "And he describes a fire burial used in ancient rituals."

"He had a thing about burials."

"Dad was a poet," she said as she finished the last of her grits. "Many deep thinkers have a fascination with death and dying."

He drained his coffee, and they set out for the Greenwell Law Firm on the other side of the square. The three-story brick building stood beside the one movie theater in town that specialized in oldies and art films. There had been talk of establishing a Tremont film festival using some of the celebrity patrons from Aspen for promotion.

In spite of the humble exterior, the furnishings on the second-floor offices were lush and expensive-looking. Ty suspected their law practice was lucrative. There wasn't much crime in Tremont County, but legal services were required for real estate, property transfers and sales that ranged from a broken-down John Deere tractor to an original Brancusi sculpture.

He recognized the receptionist, a recently divorced woman named Luann who dated one of his deputies. He introduced her to Vanessa. "We're here for our appointment with Denny Nussbaum."

She looked up from her computer screen. "I heard that Mr. Nussbaum went to grade school with Miss Whitman."

"It's Vanessa," she said. "And I remember Denny."

He realized that she was holding back information, not betraying her feelings—whether negative or positive—about the lawyer. Ty moved back a step, waiting to see how this reunion played out. He had no reason to be suspicious of the lawyer, but Nussbaum's behavior seemed odd and strangely distant. If his firm had information about the Whitman family, why hadn't he contacted her?

Denny Nussbaum charged through a dark-stained door and rushed toward Vanessa as though he were a very busy, important man. He greeted her with a painfully awkward hug. "I was sorry to hear about your father."

"Thank you."

He guided them into his office. After telling the receptionist to hold his calls, Denny dove behind his massive desk and gestured for them to sit opposite him in carved antique-looking chairs. "Vanessa, I've thought about you many times. My dad has been one of your father's attorneys for over twenty years. He worked with Dorothy longer than that."

"I'm really hoping you can help me."

"Anything," he said expansively. "I've got to admit that I feel guilty about the way our firm allowed your father to divest himself of assets. John Whitman was just throwing his money away. When he decided to do something, he wouldn't listen to advice. Trips to the South Pacific. Investing in a seat on a space shuttle. He was quite a character. Am I right?"

She nodded.

"I remember one time," Nussbaum said, "when he ran out of cash in Reno and sold one of Dorothy's favorite horses. Lucky he won the animal back. She would have killed him."

"Uh-huh."

"He managed to pull this scam off without

speaking to her. Your father was charming, eccentric and irresponsible."

Ty could see Vanessa's anger rising. Her cheeks reddened. Her slender fingers clenched into tight fists. Nussbaum was oblivious to her mood. He'd grown into a tall man with skinny shoulders, a flabby gut and a desperate need to prove he was a winner.

Vanessa interrupted his monologue. "Excuse me, Denny. You're aware that Dad had been dying of cancer for the past four years, aren't you?"

"And I'm very sorry."

"He invested most of those liquidated assets in experimental medical treatments, hoping he could save his own life. And I would have paid ten times that amount if there had been a sliver of a chance." She fought to keep her lip from quivering. "If you don't mind, I'd rather not reminisce. I have a few questions. Then you can get back to your busy day."

"Of course."

"Twenty years ago, there was a split between Dad and Dorothy. After that, Dad and Mom and I left the Castle and never moved back. Can you tell me anything about the estrangement?"

"It involved inheritance and the way the

family funds would be dispersed." He gave a smug little smile. "I don't know if it's ethical to reveal the documents."

Vanessa surged to her feet. "If you can't help, tell me who in this law firm will explain the Whitman family documents."

"Settle down."

She braced her hands on the desk. Ty wouldn't have been surprised if she leaped over the in-box and throttled him. "Don't tell me to settle down."

Nussbaum stood and stuck out his pointy chin. "What are you going to do? Punch me in the face? That's your solution to everything."

Ty feared this confrontation would erupt into violence, and he inserted himself into the fray. "Excuse me, Mr. Nussbaum. Does your father still work for Greenwell Law Firm?"

"He's a partner. So what?"

"Vanessa might prefer talking to him."

Nussbaum backed down. "He's not in."

"We'll wait." Vanessa turned on her heel and marched toward the door. "Good day, Denny."

"No, no, no, no." He scampered around his desk and closed the door to his office. "I'll tell you anything."

Without facing him, she said, "The split between Dad and Dorothy. Why?"

"It was about money, the family inheritance." He touched her arm. "I'm sorry."

"Apology accepted." She returned to her chair. "These things happened a long time ago. Are you familiar with the details?"

"I started looking into the Whitman file about six months ago." He returned to his throne behind the desk and removed a file from a drawer. "This is a summary that I prepared for Lowell Burke, Bethany's husband."

"Why?"

"Due diligence. Burke was working with Yuri Kirov to determine if selling off pieces of the Simplicity empire was a solid investment. Many of their questions referred to the Castle. They wanted to know if you or your father had any claim or any share in the ownership. You don't. Not at all. Again, I'm sorry and wish I had better news."

Ty was starting to put the pieces together. Six months ago, Vanessa was being menaced by a stalker. It couldn't be a coincidence that the Burke–Kirov due diligence started at the same time.

She shrugged. "I never thought I owned the Castle."

"About that split twenty years ago," Nussbaum said. "I studied many of my father's old cases but could never bring myself to look at this one. When you and your family left, I turned my back on all things Whitman. Somehow, I always thought we'd make up and be friends again."

Ty felt bad for both of them. Bethany's murder was only part of the investigation. To truly understand what happened, Vanessa had to travel back in time and face her past.

"I missed you, too," she said, "and I want to mend fences after this investigation is over."

"Okay." He flipped open the file folder. "Your family has many weird provisions about inheritance. To make a long story short, this is how it works. One sibling inherits all the property with the understanding that the other relatives would be compensated. Since Dorothy was the eldest child, she got all tangible property and the responsibility that went with it."

The arrangement made sense to Ty, especially since Dorothy was levelheaded and her brother was flighty. She was the nester. He was the exotic bird.

Nussbaum continued, "Your dad wanted to buy an island in the Caribbean. Dorothy refused to loosen up that much money. He insisted on a split where they never had to consult with each other again. Simon, her beloved spouse, would inherit all property. I like to think that Dorothy and John would have made up, but there were other big life events: your mom's death, Simon's success with Simplicity, your departure for college."

"Me?" She looked from Nussbaum to Ty and back again. "I didn't think Dorothy paid attention to me and what was happening in my life."

"She adored you, Vanessa. She went to your graduation in a disguise and applauded every award you won." He reached into the folder and produced a codicil to Dorothy's last will and testament. "She wanted to make sure you were always taken care of, and she didn't trust her brother to make that happen. Rather than give an inheritance in property, she took out a life insurance policy worth four mil. You're the sole beneficiary."

And her suicide negated the payout.

Chapter Seventeen

After Vanessa promised to visit Denny Nussbaum and meet his wife, she and Ty left the Greenwell Law Firm and got into his patrol car. While he drove around the square and headed toward the highway, one word echoed in her head—*why?*

Why had Aunt Dorothy committed suicide? Her life wasn't miserable. She and Simon had loved each other a lot. Why kill herself? Supposedly, when she was contemplating suicide, she'd been making plans for Christmas and sewing herself a fancy gown for the Ski Ball. It just didn't make sense.

Vanessa lowered the window and dangled her hand in the autumn breeze. "Why suicide?"

"Maybe it wasn't," Ty said.

"Doc signed the death certificate. Cause of death—suicide. Why would he do that if it weren't true?" She remembered her conversation with him. "He felt terrible about telling Simon that his wife killed herself."

"Doc could have made a mistake."

"Somebody would have noticed," she said. "Other people viewed the remains. Keith Gable was with him constantly. And, again, why? Why would anyone want her death to be suicide?"

"I can't think of any motivation, except for the insurance company trying to avoid the payout."

"Far-fetched." She reached into her backpack and found her list, which she'd revised and made more specific since last night. "Before we start with the drone, I need to stop at the Castle."

"Works for me," he said. "I was going to suggest that we start our search at the Castle, anyway. If we follow the steps in the story, young Dorothy and your dad set out from that place."

The first descriptive passage referred to the plaintive cries of other barn cats in mourning, a broken wheelbarrow and the scent of hay and apples. "The first step on their funeral procession could be the horse barn."

"And I should check in with Morris. He's

figured out a couple of ways the murderer got into and out of the locked room. And he ought to have autopsy results."

She'd been so focused on Aunt Dorothy's cold case that Bethany's murder had faded into the shadows in the back of her mind. "If Burke is at the Castle, I wouldn't mind talking to him."

"According to Nussbaum, Burke is the one who got the ball rolling six months ago when he started due diligence for Yuri Kirov. I doubt that Burke is going to give us any new info."

"You're probably right. The timing is interesting. Six months ago, the stalker started following me."

"He might have gotten the idea that you knew something about the property that could ruin the sale. But Nussbaum didn't mention any connection." He glanced over at her. "I'm glad you and Denny reconciled."

"For a while, I didn't think we'd have such a happy ending. He was being a jerk, right? I would have been justified in smacking him."

"As an officer of the law, I don't advocate violence as a solution, but yeah. He was being a jerk."

"His ears don't look as big as I remembered. Do you think he had plastic surgery?"

"Maybe he just grew into them."

"Nobody likes the way they looked as a kid. I hated, I mean really hated, my freckles."

He drove the SUV onto a wide road with a ditch along one side. At the third house, he pulled into the driveway. "Here's where we get the drone," he said. "Come inside with me."

"I'd rather stay in the car."

"That's not how this works," he said as he parked. "When you got shot yesterday, I became your bodyguard. You don't go anywhere without me."

"You're being a tiny bit overprotective. I'll be in the car, ten paces away from the front door."

"Not safe. I don't have bulletproof glass in the windshield." He exited from the SUV, came around to her side and opened the door. "Let's go."

She followed him inside where he introduced her to the man who ran the S&R operation for the wilderness area in Tremont and Pitkin counties. Though Vanessa didn't feel sociable, she managed to be polite. Proper behavior was as much a part of her as her last name.

Before they left, Ty stowed the drone in the rear of the SUV. It was in a cardboard box and not very heavy from the way he was carrying the box. She wasn't a big fan of new technology, but Vanessa was fascinated with the drone. Flying through the forest and gathering information with a tiny camera seemed impossibly cool.

"Is it hard to use?" she asked.

"Not when I have it synched up with the GPS on my phone. You'll get your turn, but don't tell anybody else that we're running a search with a drone."

"Because it's dangerous for too many people to know?"

"It's not so much about the danger," he said. "It's the fun factor. I don't want a lot of people playing with this piece of equipment."

He parked on the lowest level outside the Castle, locked his vehicle and they hiked up the winding staircase to a side entrance that she could access with her card. As soon as the door opened, she was hit with the spicy fragrance of veggie stir-fry, sweet and sour chicken and deep-fried egg rolls. In the kitchen, several woks were sizzling and steaming. According to Simon, these recipes weren't authentic Chinese. Vanessa didn't care. She preferred the Americanized version.

"Wish I hadn't eaten such a big breakfast," she said.

"There's always room for more." Ty followed his nose into the kitchen, where Mona intercepted him and rushed around preparing a plate for his lunch.

When she had Ty seated at a table with Morris and a few of the other agents, Mona came back to her. "Vanessa, dear, are you hungry?"

"Not right now." She scooped a fortune cookie from a bowl on the counter. "I'll just grab a little snack."

"Don't bother reading the fortune." Mona smoothed her pinstriped apron. "I can tell you what it says."

"Is that so? Are you psychic?"

"Just observant." She pressed her fingers to her temples. "Your fortune is that you've found the man of your dreams, and you're going to live happily-ever-after."

Vanessa looked toward the door to the dining area and saw Ty standing there with an odd expression on his face. She opened her cookie and read, "I will take a trip across distant waters."

Mona huffed. "I like mine better."

"But the trip is a possible scenario." Dad wanted his ashes spread in three locations— by the grave of her mother, in the mountains and in an ocean where they could spread to exotic locales. "I was planning a trip to a beach in northern California with a historic lighthouse that gets cut off by the rising waters of high tide."

"I know that beach," Ty murmured.

Had she spoken of the place before? Or were they connected on a deeper level. "It's been said that mermaids live there."

Behind her back, she heard Keith Gable scoff. "Another fairy tale? You need to think about the real world, Vanessa."

"I didn't ask for your advice."

"But you need it," he said. "How come you moved out of the Castle?"

"Yesterday, somebody tried to kill me."

"Are you sure this isn't another fairy tale?"

"The sheriff doesn't think so. He wants me in protective custody." He wanted her in his bed, and that was where she intended to stay.

"Well, I hope he can put you on the right path. You're wasting time with stories about what happened to Dorothy. It's done. Settled. Move on."

He was so smug. Unfortunately, he was one of the few people who had been close to Simon and Dorothy at the time of her disappearance. Vanessa couldn't just come out and ask direct questions about that time because Keith had no motivation to cooperate with her.

She used a research interview tactic to keep him talking: make the conversation all about him. "When you and Simon launched the Simple Simon's franchise, the gourmet restaurant was faltering. It might be said that you saved the day."

"That's what I mean about living in the real world. The franchises were my dream, but it took hard work and smart marketing to make my concept a success."

There was no lack of ego on his part. Over the years, Keith and Simon had argued in epic battles. Vanessa had researched some of their feuds for the memoir but probably wouldn't use them in the book. Simon wanted to protect his image as a brilliant chef who only cared about the food. She wondered how Keith felt about Aunt Dorothy. He had to stay on her good side. After all, her property financed his franchises.

"Aunt Dorothy's death wasn't a fairy tale," she said. "Her body was mangled by predators, and she died alone."

Before she could delve more deeply into the dark tragedy, Ty stepped up beside her and carefully guided her away from a conversation that might turn explosive. She didn't trust Keith, but she couldn't for the life of her think of a reason why Dorothy's death by suicide would help him.

In a low voice, she asked Ty, "Am I turning into a loose cannon? It seems like I'm running around with a lit fuse, looking for trouble."

"Are you?"

"I'm frustrated. None of these pieces of evidence seem to fit."

"We need an expert," he said. "Agent Morris called in the best."

At the table where he had been sitting with the other agents, Ty introduced her to Dr. Emily Waters, a forensic pathologist based in Aspen. "Dr. Waters observed Bethany's autopsy at the CBI facility in Denver."

Vanessa shook her hand. "Was any new information discovered?"

"Not yet." She had a lovely white smile and a pleasant bedside manner that was totally wasted on the deceased. "Cause of death was blunt force trauma to the skull. No drugs in her system. I wanted to come back here and look into her living situation and possible environmental factors that might have played into her death."

"I've worked with Dr. Waters before," Morris said. "She sees things that most people—including me—are prone to overlook."

"Which is why she can help us," Ty said. "If we can locate Dorothy's remains, we'll have access to all kinds of details about how she died, how long her body was exposed to the elements and what kind of animals gnawed on her bones."

Vanessa was impressed. "You can do that?"

"The dead hold on to their secrets. I looked over the autopsy notes from Dr. Ingram, which were vague and inconclusive. I would have liked to have seen X-rays and photographs."

Now, Vanessa was even more motivated to get on with the search. Finding Aunt Dorothy's remains was significant, and it felt good to be taken seriously by an expert. "We'll be in touch."

In spite of Ty's earlier insistence not to add anyone to the search party, he had assembled a small group, including a deputy to help them dig up the remains and the short-haired female agent who was an expert in all things electronic. Vanessa took out her notebook and checked her list. There was one more thing she needed to do before they set out.

She squeezed Ty's arm. "I'll be right back."

In the Grand Hall, she took the staircase to the third-floor library. Her area hadn't been marked off with crime scene tape like the master bedroom directly below, but the door was closed. She looked over her shoulder and saw Ty following. "What are you doing here?" she asked.

"I don't want to get in your way," he said, "but I've got to keep you safe. That means watching, constantly."

Being protected wasn't her idea of a good time, but she'd be foolish to ignore him. "I'll try not to go running off."

She pivoted. Using her key, she unlocked the library and entered. Though she was aware of Ty following behind her, she whispered as she took the urn from the shelf and placed it on the long table with the carved legs.

"Hi, Dad, it's Vanessa. We're almost finished with the search for Aunt Dorothy. You chose her final resting place so it must be important. That's where I'm going to scatter another portion of your ashes. To honor your memory and our family."

She'd learned a lot about the eccentric Whitmans, and she felt a renewed kinship, almost wished she'd taken the time to know Bethany better.

She grasped the urn in her hand and tightened the lid. The metal surface should have been cold but it was as warm as a living thing. Dad was here with her. Even when his ashes were gone, he'd be a part of her.

Chapter Eighteen

It was Ty's turn to be organized, and he relied on his ability to delegate. He used experts to work on the drone search. Vanessa the English teacher took charge of interpreting her father's prose, turning the story of Fluffball's funeral into a metaphorical map. Deputy Randall carried a rifle over his shoulder and was on guard against possible sabotage or ambush. Most useful was the federal agent named Liz Hurtado, who expertly operated the Phantom 4 Pro video camera drone. Ty had experience and could drive drones that were basically kids' toys, scanning an area from above. The professional level was far more complex.

Following the Mr. Fluffball narrative, they drove to the horse barn and hiked downhill to a creek. In this early autumn season, there was only a narrow trickle of water and wide banks that Vanessa's father had described as pillows of sand and mud. According to his narrative, the route of their funeral procession went south toward the twin summits of Mount Sopris.

"Here's where it gets vague," she said. "He describes the azure sky and the breeze and the sunlight, blah, blah, blah. Those things could be anywhere."

"Let's go to the drone," Ty said.

Agent Hurtado removed the aircraft from its box and set up her tracking equipment on the ground while she explained the mechanics of the camera, which was capable of zooming in and out while turning on a circular axis. The four synched rotating engines made it possible to hover.

"Like a helicopter," he said.

"Pretty much. And we have two extra batteries, which should give a search radius of thirty miles. That isn't as far as you might think."

"Doesn't matter," Randall said. "It's only a couple of hours before sundown. When the light fades, we won't be able to see well enough to continue. Say, do you think I could take the drone home to show my four-year-old daughter?"

"Check with the guys at Search and Rescue," Ty said.

Hurtado cleared her throat and adjusted her collar. "Does your daughter like electronics?"

"You bet! She knows more about the computer than I do."

"If you get the okay," Hurtado said, "I'd be happy to show her the basics of drones. The world needs more women in my field."

"Thank you, ma'am."

"Prepared for takeoff?" Hurtado asked.

Ty bobbed his head. When he glanced over at Vanessa, he recognized the excitement that flushed her cheeks beneath her freckles. She clutched her dad's book and stared at the futuristic drone as it hummed to life, lifted off and hovered about four feet off the ground.

Hurtado had plugged the operating system into her phone to access the GPS and other data. "Does it save the video?" Vanessa asked.

"It does. Do you want to take it for a spin?"

"Oh, yeah." Seated on the ground by Hurtado, Vanessa practiced the basic drone moves and then—predictably—she accelerated and swooped. Talk about an exotic bird! Laughing, she made a wild dive and circled his head, coming close enough that she bumped his hat off his head.

"Let's get started with the search," Hurtado said as she reclaimed the controls. Her guidance was excellent as she swept from left to right and back again.

Ty was amazed by the clarity of the video and the detail that could be seen from a great height. "Can you go lower?"

"It's hard to find the sweet spot, staying high enough that the rotors don't get tangled in the tree branches but low enough to see what's on the ground."

"This is what we're looking for." He handed her the Polaroid of the homemade tombstone for the yellow cat. After all this time, a lot could have changed. If the paint wasn't the indelible type, it might have washed away. Or the stone might have blown down or been buried under a fallen tree.

"Look at this," Vanessa said as she leaned close to the screen. "It's a fire circle. There's no way of figuring out how old it is, but the Fluffball story talks about playing *Kumbaya* on the guitar in front of a fire. Should we go closer?"

He didn't want to have her exposed to a shooter while she tromped through the forest unprotected. "Your dad was only a kid when they buried the cat. How would he know about playing a guitar?"

"In this story, time drifts in and out. He arranges the context to suit the message."

"How do you know about this stuff?"

"Writing was something I shared with Dad."

He understood. Ty and his dad both enjoyed hunting and spent endless hours in the hills and forests of Montana, tracking and hiking. Some days, they went hours without speaking. Didn't need to. And neither of them liked to end the hunt with a kill. When they bagged a deer or an elk, they used every part of the animal.

He and his dad were alike in many ways. They were both practical, both nesters.

Hurtado made an adjustment on the tracking screen. "I'm going into the forest to search and need to be careful. Otherwise, I'll get hung up on a tree."

"Can you give us a wide shot?" Ty asked.

"Higher than three hundred feet, and we'll start to lose focus, but I can give you a bird's eye angle."

The drone swept over the forest, hovering above spaces that were too difficult to explore. In a large rock formation that reminded him of the Hag Stone, they spotted the entrance to a cave. Coming back toward the creek, the drone zipped around groves and thickets. This part of the forest was relatively dense. "It doesn't look like there's been a fire around here in ages."

"Not this close to the Castle," Vanessa said. "I heard there was a fire last night. From the lightning. A tree on the ridge burned."

"We're lucky it didn't spread."

After swooping and circling and hovering, Hurtado guided the drone back to where they'd stationed themselves so she could change the battery. Checking her GPS maps, she pointed out the area they'd covered. "We went right from here. Now we'll try the other direction."

He watched Vanessa lean back against a rock and stretch her arms over her head in a yawn. She was flexible. Like a cat. He sat beside her, enjoying the quiet of the forest and wishing their search was over. He wanted to take her home with him and spend the night in her arms. When this investigation was over, he didn't want to deliver her back to the Castle.

"Have you thought about what you want to do when we wrap up Bethany's murder?"

"*If* we wrap it up," she said. "What do you think, Agent Hurtado? Is Morris any closer to finding the killer?"

"We still haven't located Bethany's lover," she said. "But I think Yuri Kirov might be first in line for having an affair with her. Before he married Macy, he had a reputation for being a playboy. And it was his glove you found on the Hag Stone."

"I think the glove was planted," Ty said.

"Or maybe Yuri dropped it," Hurtado said. "If not Yuri, I'm leaning toward the husband. He's a shifty character, and I'm not just saying that because he's a lawyer. There's something about Bethany claiming that they were going to be millionaires that makes me want to take another look at him."

She finished replacing the battery and launched the drone again.

He turned toward Vanessa who was gazing at him with a glimmer of curiosity in her dark brown eyes. "Why did you ask about my plans?"

"I thought after all these situations, you might not want to stay at the Castle."

She nodded. "I'm committed to staying

here and finishing the book for Simon. We signed a contract, and he's paying me decent money."

"And you like being a ghost."

"True, I like being a ghost, but you're right about the Castle. It's uncomfortable…and dangerous."

This was the opening he'd hoped for. He could make the offer for her to stay with him until the book was done. His schedule meant he'd be gone most of the time. She'd have plenty of time and space. "This might be too soon to ask, but…"

"Take a look," Hurtado said. "I'm seeing an object that doesn't belong in the forest. It's bright yellow."

He bounced to his feet and squinted at the screen. "It's the edge of the gravestone. Can you zoom in?"

She adjusted the focus, and the burial place for Mr. Fluffball came into view. Vanessa did a victory dance and threw her good arm around him for a hug. "We did it!"

They'd found the cat. Now, where was Dorothy?

Ty gathered his little group together, and they set out to find the physical location of the yellow tombstone. Vanessa was so excited that she dragged them off course three times even though Hurtado indicated the path they should follow with GPS coordinates. Uphill from the creek, they crossed a field of rocks that Vanessa said looked like Stonehenge. Score another landmark point for her dad! From there, they went into a wooded glen. The burial ground for Mr. Fluffball wasn't hidden but it wasn't obvious. There weren't many people who went hiking or had picnics on this land so close to the Castle, and he couldn't think of another reason anyone would come here. This was private property with no hunting allowed. Not suitable for recreation. Too much forest for an ATV.

Vanessa darted up to the grave marker with yellow painted edges and read the black inscription. *Mr. Fluffball. Silly cat. Rest in peace.* She dropped to her knees and reached out, touching the painted letters with her fingers. "I never knew this animal. He was long dead before I was born, but I feel that Fluffball is part of my heritage, a symbol of my weird family. Dad thought enough of the Fluffball funeral that he wrote a story about it."

"One problem," Ty said. "We're not looking for a cat. It's Dorothy we need to find."

With a whoosh, she emptied her lungs of air and sank to the ground in front of the grave marker. "Maybe Dad was sending some kind of message."

"Like what? Too bad, suckers!"

"It's got to be buried around here. How big was the coffin?"

He had a hard time thinking of a metal box as a coffin, but he'd play along with her. What other option did he have? "Roughly the size of a carry-on suitcase."

She paced around the perimeter of the clearing. "If Dad were here, what would he say?"

"I'm not good at epitaphs," Ty said, "and I never knew either of these people. If I had to guess, I'd say that—in spite of their squabbles—they loved each other. And that's what you call ironic."

"So sad. So true. Their relationship was fraught with irony. Like an arrow that aims in a circle and never hits the mark."

Hurtado exchanged a glance with Randall. They both looked at Ty. In unison, the three of them shrugged.

"Don't you get it?" Vanessa said. "A heart and an arrow that goes around it in a circle. That's the design on the locket."

Ty had known that the necklace—which was now locked away in his gun safe at home—had a connection. The locket was the first clue that pointed toward Aunt Dorothy. "What does it mean?"

"When Dorothy assigned the task of staging her burial to Dad, he must have seen the irony. She turned to him. Even after their long estrangement, she loved her brother. The locket was a symbol of that irony."

Ty listened and nodded. "I'm going to need a little more help to figure this out."

"Everything is upside down and backward." She walked in a circle to the back side of the gravestone. A scrawl on the back was an arrow that made a circle, then pointed straight down. "Dorothy is buried here, on the flip side of Mr. Fluffball."

Ty picked up the spade and sliced into the earth. In minutes, the spade hit metal. The grave wasn't deep. He quickly and easily cleared the dirt from the box. Together, he and Randall lifted it from the hole.

The silvery box looked something like a treasure chest with fancy scrollwork on the corners and an ornate lock on the front. "It's locked," he said.

"You have a spade. Crack it open."

"No mistakes," he said. "We need to follow protocol and maintain the chain of evidence. I don't want this case to fall apart because we weren't patient enough to handle it properly."

"You're right," said Hurtado.

Randall nodded his agreement.

"I'm the only person who isn't an active member of law enforcement," Vanessa said. "What are we supposed to do?"

Though his fingers were itching to rip apart the box, Ty wasn't going to make a mistake. This whole story was already far-fetched. He didn't need complications. "We turn the box over to Dr. Waters, the forensic pathologist. She can either use some kind of X-ray machine or open the box under supervision. She'll contact us with her findings."

"That doesn't sound so bad." Vanessa gazed up at him. "There's something I need to do. Can I have a moment?"

He reached into her backpack, took out the urn and handed it to her. "This is the place you've been looking for, the place where you want to scatter your father's ashes."

"He should be here with Aunt Dorothy and Fluffball." She took two handfuls of ashes and allowed them to sift through her fingers. Her movements were slow and respectful with a sense of ceremony. She leaned forward and patted the wildly colorful tombstone.

"It feels like I should say something."

"Up to you," he said.

She whispered, "Goodbye, silly cat."

THEY RETURNED TO the Castle where Ty turned the box over to Agent Morris. He watched Vanessa go with Mona into the kitchen and hoped she'd snag something for their dinner.

"Good work," Morris said. "I don't know if this will help us solve Bethany's murder, but it says a lot about Dorothy's disappearance and death."

"Our findings create more questions. Mainly, why did she kill herself?"

"That's the problem with cold cases. Witnesses come and go and don't usually have clear memories. The evidence is spotty at best." He studied the ornate silvery box. "Why the hell would they bury her in that thing? How come she wanted her brother to dispose of her remains instead of the beloved husband?"

Ty had a feeling about Dorothy's remains. There would be one more clue that put everything in perspective. "When do you want us here for the reenactment?"

"One o'clock. Come a little earlier and have lunch."

He didn't need to be invited twice. Ty was aware that he was treating the Castle like his own personal fast-food franchise, but he didn't feel guilty. There was always activity in the kitchen, and they had the best pantry in the state.

He and Vanessa didn't bother discussing where she'd sleep tonight. No question. She came home with him, and they celebrated their success with sandwiches made from roast beef, fancy cheese, tomatoes and lo-cally-sourced romaine lettuce. The beverage was a local craft beer that he kept on hand.

He scarfed down the sandwich in record time. "I guess I was hungrier than I thought."

"It's been a long day," she said. "Make yourself another sandwich. And try these freshly made potato chips."

"If I lived at the Castle, I'd weigh seven hundred pounds."

"It's not a good place to be on a diet."

He took a drink of the ice-cold beer and savored the full-bodied taste. "I've got to say congratulations to us, but if you weren't part of this crazy family, we never would have been able to unravel all the twists and turns."

"Now all I have to do is figure out who murdered Bethany," she said. "Do you think Agent Morris will be too upset if we outsmart him?"

"If we refer to outsmarting him, he's not going to be happy." Ty was pleased with the professional relationship he'd developed with the CBI. "There aren't many guys who like to be reminded when they aren't the smartest in the room."

"How about you?"

"I've got no problem admitting that you win the genius prize. Not that it's a contest. I'm just happy to see things from your point of view. I like to learn."

He didn't know why she beamed a smile at him but was glad she did. From the first time he met her, he liked the way they fit. Like matching pieces in a puzzle. They were comfortable together. While they ate, they talked about drones and how useful they were for search and rescue. And they spoke about the approaching ski season. And they shared long moments of silence when talking wasn't necessary.

After they cleaned up the dishes, she asked to see more of his DIY projects.

"Matter of fact," he said, "I've got something new I've been thinking about. You're kind of the inspiration for it."

"Me?"

"That's right." He led her out of the kitchen and down the hall behind the staircase to a smallish room with a window that looked out on the front porch. "I wanted this to be a gym but it's not big enough. Then, I thought I'd turn it into a guest bedroom."

She went to the window and pulled the curtain aside so she could see out. "I'm guessing this is a great view in daylight."

"And it's not bad at night." If he hadn't been concerned about her safety, he would have taken her for a moonlight stroll. "This is going to be an office. I can use lots of built-in cabinets for storage and equipment. And a computer desk over here."

"I'm not sure that's a great idea." She stepped into the center of the room and slowly turned around. "I think you could turn this into a great office, but you've got plenty of space at the courthouse. Do you really want to bring your work home with you?"

He hadn't been thinking about *his* work. Not at all. He wanted to build an office *for her* so that she could stay here while she was working on her book. Living at the Castle wouldn't be necessary. He wanted to give her something she couldn't get anywhere else. But it might be too soon to start making grand gestures. He needed to take his time and give his exotic bird a chance to spread her wings.

Last night when they made love, he'd been insanely passionate, carried away by emotions that ran deeper and stronger than anything he'd felt before. Tonight was different. They undressed for bed slowly, taking time to appreciate the view. Her breasts were high and small but not too small. Just right. Moonlight spilled through the window and outlined her slender waist.

He glided his hand along the flare of her hips and back to those beautiful breasts. When she snuggled against him, her long legs twined with his. Again, a perfect fit. Their breath was in synch. And their pulse. They finished at exactly the same time. Fulfilled.

He lay beside her under the comforter. Not talking. There were a few things he wanted to say, but he held his silence.

She ran her hand over his head. "I like the way your hair feels."

"Back at you."

"Would you like to join me in the shower?"

"Yes, please."

He wanted to tell her that he loved her. Those words had been building inside him from the first time he heard her voice and saw her face. But he knew she wasn't ready. Those words were pretty much the worst thing he could say.

Chapter Nineteen

Vanessa woke with a sense of tension and trouble. Something was wrong with their relationship. Was that what she should call this? A relationship? She hated to pin down the complex emotions she'd shared with Ty. One word didn't suffice.

Before she got out of bed, she put in a call to Dr. Waters's office to find out if they'd opened the box or started the odd autopsy on a skull and a couple of old bones. The doctor's assistant gave Vanessa a brief but condescending lecture on the equipment they'd use and promised to have Dr. Waters call back as soon as possible. Vanessa threw on a T-shirt and jeans and padded barefooted down the staircase.

Ty had already made coffee and heated the morning pastry unleashing delightful aromas of cinnamon and fresh brew. She plunked into a chair at the kitchen table. "I called Dr. Waters."

"Did she have any information?"

"Not yet. Her assistant mentioned something irrelevant about fluorescent spectrometer magnification. I'm going to keep calling. If there's one thing I learned from four years as Dad's caretaker, it's that squeaky wheels get the grease."

"Squeak on." He filled her mug with thick black coffee, the way he liked it. When he kissed her cheek and nibbled her ear, she almost forgot about her relationship misgivings. *Almost.*

"Do we have a plan for the day?" she asked.

"Are you going to make a list?"

"I always do."

"At one o'clock, we're supposed to go to the Castle and participate in a reenactment of the hours before Bethany's body was found."

"How precise is this supposed to be? I mean, should I wear the same clothes?"

"I don't think that's necessary, but I wouldn't mind seeing that soft blue blouse again."

"You remember what I was wearing?"

"I'm an officer of the law, trained to observe and recall details," he said. "We should get over to the Castle early so we can grab some lunch."

For a single guy like Ty, finding a constant supply of gourmet food must feel like a bonanza. "You really are a scavenger," she said.

"I ought to replenish my supplies. Maybe swing by the grocery store."

"That goes on the list," she said.

He rose from the table and grasped her hand. "Come this way and bring your coffee."

In the small room he might turn into an office, he'd done some renovating. There was a small desk, a swivel chair and a notebook. "Where did you find this stuff?"

"Garage. I thought you might need list-making supplies, and I've got a bunch of odds and ends just lying around."

He pulled a cord, and the curtain swept open. The view was as spectacular as she thought it would be. Coffee mug on the table, she sat on the chair that had already been adjusted to her height. She flipped open the notebook and picked up the pen. Her morning ritual usually started this way.

She noted the meeting at one o'clock, then she added groceries with a few basics, like bread and eggs. "What else?"

"Lumberyard," he said. "I want to pick up a couple of shelving units."

Her pen paused above the notebook. The lumberyard was the natural habitat of nesting creatures. And the shelving units were destined to end up in this room. He was building a nest for her inside the home he'd built for himself. She liked Ty, liked him a lot. But this plan was unacceptable.

She pushed back her chair and stood. "I should get ready."

"Stay. We have other items for the list. You said that you wanted to pick up some of your clothes from the Castle."

She had mentioned that. Also, she wanted the recording equipment for Simon's memoir. But she couldn't let herself be seduced into complacency by her need for organization. "You have to stop this, Ty."

"Stop what?"

He looked so innocent, but she had him figured out. "You're building me a nest."

"I want to keep you protected."

"Of course, I want that. I'm not a risk-taker. As much as I want to be like Dad, I'm not him, not spontaneous."

"What's the problem?"

"You think you're building a nest, but it feels like a birdcage to me."

The expression on his face told her that she'd hurt him, which was the opposite of what she wanted. "Believe me," he said. "I'm not trying to force you into a situation you don't want. And I'm sure as hell not locking you up in a cage."

She stalked out the door and dashed upstairs. This morning, she'd realized that they had a relationship. Already, it had blown up in her face. Was it her responsibility to apologize? That didn't seem fair.

She got dressed and practiced deep breathing until she was nearly calm. When she returned to the kitchen, she had every intention of making things right. *Stay cool. Stay steady.* She confronted him directly, determined not to be distracted by his firm jaw, handsome eyes and dimples. "Here's the thing, Ty. I'm not going to tell you that I'm sorry."

"Neither am I."

This wasn't turning out the way she wanted. They needed to have a rational conversation, maybe make a list of pros and cons. How could she be angry about his effort to help her out with a new office? And how could he assume he knew what was best for her?

She took her coffee mug to the sink and rinsed it out. Then she gathered up her backpack. "I don't think we should ride to the Castle together."

"Fine with me. I'll call a deputy to give you a ride."

Shoving open the front door, she went onto the porch and sat in a rocking chair. She called over her shoulder to him. "I'll wait out here."

No doubt, she made a pathetic picture in her wilted blouse from yesterday and her backpack holding the last third of Dad's ashes. But she wasn't going to give in. No apologies.

AT THE CASTLE, Vanessa went to her room and changed into a denim shirt. Not wanting to waste time avoiding Ty, she fixed her hair, put on makeup and called Dr. Waters, who still didn't have any news. Keeping herself busy, she stayed out of sight until right before one o'clock.

In the Grand Hall, she gathered with the others, including Ty, who was dressed in his uniform shirt and utility belt. He wasn't wearing his cowboy hat. Morris told them that they had five minutes to get to their initial starting place. "I can't expect you to follow the same precise timing but try to make it close. Any questions?"

"What's the point?" Macy demanded.

"You're all witnesses," he said. "At the time the murder occurred, you didn't know what might be significant. Reenacting the event might jog your memory."

"Sounds lame to me. We've been cooperative so far, but I think it might be time to call our attorneys and put a stop to this nonsense."

Her husband, Yuri, chided her. "A lovely young woman is dead. We will assist the police in any way we can."

Not speaking to each other, she and Ty went to the staircase and ascended to the balcony outside the crime scene on the second floor. Agent Hurtado had been chosen to play the role of Bethany. She charged past them, entered Simon's bedroom and locked the door.

Instead of following the same path they'd walked before, Vanessa looked to see whom "Bethany" had been arguing with before she locked herself in. Lowell Burke, her husband, stood in the hallway.

"That's how it started," she said to Ty.

"They argued about money. She said something about millions of dollars."

"We don't know the details, but Burke was investigating property rights and entanglements on Simplicity and with the Simple Simon's franchises."

She remembered the timing. Six months ago, Burke's investigation started and that was about the time she was aware of being stalked in Denver. "Do we think Burke is the stalker?"

"Could be. He's got a sneaky side."

She looked down from the balcony. It felt good to be talking to Ty again. She leaned against the second floor railing, trying to remember whom she'd seen in the Grand Hall. Chloe Markham? Mona? Keith must have been down there because she saw him heading toward the bakery kitchen on the first floor.

"Keith Gable," Ty said. "He's also involved in the sale of the property. He's a partner with Simon."

"Sounds like everybody has their fingers in that pie."

Together, she and Ty crossed the Grand Hall to the other side. They went past the office with the French doors. At the staircase, she'd mentioned the movie room on the lower level but they never went there. On the second floor, they ran into Martha Ingram who was trying to act like she was upset.

"If you don't mind having me ask," Ty said, "what was bothering you the first time we saw you?"

"It's George. He's drinking too much. Hasn't been feeling well."

"Sorry to hear that," Ty said.

"He's been having nightmares. He wakes up in a cold sweat and mumbles about being sorry, so very sorry." Her gaze darted nervously toward him. "Once, I heard him apologize to you in his sleep."

After she left them, Ty and Vanessa meandered up and down the staircase. "I'm glad we're friends again," she said.

"More than friends." He caught hold of her hand and squeezed gently. "So what do you think about all these suspects."

"Don't you mean witnesses? Someone in the Castle killed Bethany."

And they weren't picking up any new clues. They didn't see anyone else until they crossed the Grand Hall again and entered the second floor game room with the secret passage.

Burke was waiting for them. "Macy is right. This is a waste of time."

"Maybe not," Ty said. "Did you discover anything unusual when you were looking into property issues from twelve years ago?"

"When Aunt Dorothy disappeared?" He scoffed. "I can't betray my client's confidential information, but I didn't uncover any deep dark secrets. Nothing but innuendo. For some reason, Bethany was convinced that Dorothy wanted to give her a fortune. I think she might have met the woman once or twice but that was all."

Vanessa's phone rang. When she saw the call was coming from Dr. Waters, she answered. The pathologist gave a short, sweet and horrifying explanation of what she'd discovered in the tiny coffin box: Aunt Dorothy was murdered.

Forensics showed that she was shot in the back of the head at an angle that would have been impossible for her to pull the trigger. Vanessa rushed to rejoin Ty and Burke.

"Excuse us," she said to Bethany's husband. "We need to confer."

"Not a problem," he said. "I'm supposed to find Keith, anyway."

As soon as he was out of earshot, she told

Ty about the report. "It was murder, and that explains the motivation. Why fake a suicide? To cover up a murder."

"But Doc Ingram said suicide was the cause of death. Why did he lie?"

The door to the game room slammed shut. They were trapped.

Keith Gable stalked into the center of the room, shoving Doc in front of him. "Poor old Doc Ingram," he said with a sneer. "He's been falling apart for years."

When Ty reached for his gun, Keith raised his weapon. "Drop it, Sheriff. Do it. Or I'll shoot Vanessa first. Then the Doc."

When Ty was disarmed, Keith pushed the old man to the floor. Vanessa went to help him. "You won't get away with this, Keith."

"The hell I won't. Here's a neat little story for Morris. Doc killed Dorothy and filled in the phony cause of death. Maybe I can weave in a side issue about Doc's grandson and the drugs he's been taking. There's plenty of crimes floating around to keep any jury amused. Doc will be blamed for the whole thing."

"I would never hurt Dorothy," Doc said. "When Dorothy disappeared, I was confused and scared and I couldn't see worth a damn.

Finally, when her body showed up and I examined her, all I saw was the gunshot to the head. Keith convinced me that it was suicide."

Vanessa glared at Keith. "You're good at playing tricks on people. You're the one who stalked me, aren't you?"

"I thought I could scare you off."

"But I don't scare so easily. Tell me, Keith, when did you figure out that you'd made a mistake by killing Dorothy?"

"Not for years," he said. "You didn't seem to know anything about the insurance. Then Lowell Burke started poking around. That was when I struck up an affair with Bethany. She handed me all the information."

Keith's smarmy grin disgusted Ty. "Proud of yourself?"

"A little bit." He shrugged. "Dorothy had to die. She was standing in the way of progress. Simon and I needed free rein in leveraging the properties and starting our franchise stores. We were brilliant. The only person who didn't applaud was Dorothy. She didn't believe in me...or her husband."

"When Bethany figured out your plot," Ty said, "you couldn't have her running around with that much leverage in her back pocket."

"I seduced her, tried to show her she was

wrong, but she loved money more. Now, all that's left for me to do is clean up you three witnesses. As soon as Morris figures out that Dorothy's death was murder and Doc lied on the death certificate, he'll jump to the obvious conclusion."

"One more question," Vanessa asked, "How did you get into and out of Simon's bedroom?"

"Simple Simon." He chuckled at his own cleverness. "I went to the library and climbed down the wall. And I disposed of my blood-stained chef jacket in the laundry."

"Killing us won't be easy," Vanessa warned. "There are cops and agents swarming all over the place. They'll hear a gunshot."

"Give me some credit. I'm smarter than that." He gestured toward the pinball machines in the corner. "I want all three of you in the secret passage."

As soon as she ducked inside, Vanessa smelled gasoline. Keith intended to light the passage on fire and let it spread to the wine cellar.

Ty followed behind her. "Run. Get out of here as fast as you can."

"What about you? And Doc?"

"I'll take care of this," Doc said. "Tell Simon I'm sorry."

The old man lunged at Keith. Doc wasn't strong and wasn't in good health but he always carried a lucky scalpel in his pocket. He unsheathed the surgical blade and stabbed Keith's leg.

Vanessa hit the cement floor of the wine cellar in seconds. Ty followed. When he burst out the door behind her, Keith fired his weapon. The spark from his gun ignited the gas.

There wasn't time to rescue Doc from the explosion.

His nightmares were over.

Epilogue

Three weeks later, Vanessa stood on Crescent City Beach in California and watched as the tide ebbed. A rocky path emerged from the waters and provided a way to walk from the sandy beach to the small lighthouse island, about fifty feet offshore.

Every day for the past week, she'd come here at low tide to wait for Ty. They hadn't resolved their issues about nesting and living a more exotic life. There would always be conflicts, but she truly enjoyed the makeup sex. She was willing to try a relationship. If he wanted to try, he'd come here by the end of the day.

Her life had changed drastically since the day of the fire at the Castle. For one thing, Nussbaum had secured her insurance payout with interest, making her a wealthy woman. She'd decided to continue on the project with

Simon if he promised to give a full chapter to Aunt Dorothy. And she'd bought a cat and named it Fluff the Second.

Simon was coping pretty well with the news that his friend and partner, Keith, had murdered his beloved Dorothy. This would have been a good time to retire from the restaurant business. Instead, he doubled down, bringing in his current wife, Chloe, to run the Simple Simon franchise.

Vanessa reached up and touched the necklace that Bethany held when she was murdered. The design had turned out to be a useful clue. Even in death, Bethany had aimed focus at Aunt Dorothy. Ty never should have hidden that piece of evidence from Morris, but she was glad he did. The CBI agent might have dismissed the necklace. Bethany's dream of a huge inheritance wasn't exactly true. She'd get something. Her husband— Lowell the lawyer—would make sure of that. But Bethany hadn't been first generation, and her claim was further down the list.

From the top of the lighthouse, Vanessa stared toward the south. In the distance, she saw him approaching. A man on horseback, riding at the edge of the sparkling surf.

She climbed down the stairs from the lighthouse and dashed across the sand. When he was close enough for her to see the shimmer in his eyes, he leaned down and scooped her off her feet. She sat on his lap in the saddle. They kissed for a very long time.

"Marry me, Vanessa."

"I can't say yes to that. Not yet." She kissed him again. "But I can say I love you."

"That'll do."

* * * * *

Get 4 FREE REWARDS!

We'll send you 2 FREE Books <u>plus</u> 2 FREE Mystery Gifts.

Harlequin Romantic Suspense books are heart-racing page-turners with unexpected plot twists and irresistible chemistry that will keep you guessing to the very end.

FREE Value Over $20

Get 4 FREE REWARDS!

We'll send you 2 FREE Books plus 2 FREE Mystery Gifts.

Harlequin Presents books feature the glamorous lives of royals and billionaires in a world of exotic locations, where passion knows no bounds.

FREE
Value Over
$20